The Cuffer Anthology
VOLUME V

A Selection of Short Fiction
from Newfoundland and Labrador

Edited by Pam Frampton

© 2013, Pam Frampton

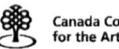 

We gratefully acknowledge the financial support of the Canada Council for the Arts, the Government of Canada through the Canada Book Fund (CBF), and the Government of Newfoundland and Labrador through the Department of Tourism, Culture and Recreation for our publishing program.

All rights reserved. No part of this work covered by the copyrights hereon may be reproduced or used in any form or by any means—graphic, electronic or mechanical—without the prior written permission of the publisher. Any requests for photocopying, recording, taping or information storage and retrieval systems of any part of this book shall be directed in writing to the Canadian Reprography Collective, One Yonge Street, Suite 1900, Toronto, Ontario M5E 1E5.

Printed on acid-free paper
Cover Design by Todd Manning
Layout by Joanne Snook-Hann

Published by
KILLICK PRESS
an imprint of CREATIVE BOOK PUBLISHING
a Transcontinental Inc. associated company
P.O. Box 8660, Stn. A
St. John's, Newfoundland and Labrador A1B 3T7

Printed in Canada

Library and Archives Canada Cataloguing in Publication

The Cuffer anthology. Volume V / Pam Frampton, editor.

ISBN 978-1-77103-021-2 (pbk.)

1. Short stories, Canadian (English)--Newfoundland and Labrador. 2. Canadian fiction (English)--21st century. 3. Newfoundland and Labrador--Fiction. I. Frampton, Pam, editor of compilation

PS8329.5.N3C835 2013   C813'.01089718   C2013-905570-3

The Cuffer Anthology
VOLUME V

A Selection of Short Fiction
from Newfoundland and Labrador

Edited by Pam Frampton

St. John's, Newfoundland and Labrador
2013

Cuffer Anthology Volume V

Introduction vii
Nancy Drew By Wanda Nolan 1
Satsuma and Cigarettes By Joshua Goudie 3
Bliss By Janet Kelly 7
Two-Man Tent By Robert Chafe 11
Unloving You By Annette Conway 15
Being Frank By Randy Drover 19
Judy McDermid's Garden of Faeries By Jamie Fitzpatrick 23
Foreshore By Joshua Goudie 27
Slideshow By Dara Squires 31
The Nightingale By Paul Whittle 35
Before There Was Air By Robert Chafe 39
Coming Home By Amanda Stephen 43
Home By Elizabeth Wright 47
I Don't Dream of Genie By Chad Pelley 53
Just Wait Till I Tells You By Michael Finn 57
Leaving By Deborah Whelan 61
Loss of the Aeolus By Ian Hutchings 65
My Candy Girl By Scott Bartlett 69
Reconciliation By Mary Pike 75
Sculpins By Dara Squires 81
Cat's Paw By Harold N. Walters 85
Fire Balloon By Scott Bartlett 91
Gum By Melanie Oates 99
Heart of the Matter By Jacquie S. Fleming 105
Killing With Kindness By Dolores Hynes 109
Lady Slipper By Paul Whittle 113
Smoke Rings By Frank Barry 119
The Countdown By Mike Daly 125
The Dumpers By Robin Reid 131
The End of the World By Jacqueline Clarke 135
Come Home Year By Nathan Downey 139
Mercy By Grant Loveys 143
Snares By Michael Finn 147
The Fates By Adrienne King 153
The Grocery List By Melissa Barbeau 157
About the Editor 163

INTRODUCTION

When the Cuffer Prize was launched five years ago, those of us behind it did not dream we would ever get to the point where choosing short stories for the annual anthology would be such a difficult process.

As with any publication, space is a consideration, so the dilemma has become what to leave in, what to leave out?

The Cuffer Anthology: Volume V contains 35 of the best stories from the 2012 Cuffer Prize competition. The breadth and depth of creativity and talent on display here is something to behold.

Within this slim volume you will find love and heartache, grief and murderous intent, devotion and despair. The stories may be short — 1,200 words or less — but they are fulsome in the lives and the worlds and the emotions they contain.

Every year since The Telegram and Creative Book Publishing started publishing this annual anthology, certain themes have mysteriously emerged in the stories. They're all set in Newfoundland and Labrador, of course, but that leaves plenty of scope for imagination — one story could be about rural life in the 1920s, while another might foresee a time and way of life farther into the future than most of us can fathom. Still, common threads can be found. Chief among them in this anthology is the idea of loss and losing oneself.

In Wanda Nolan's 1st-place winning story, *Nancy Drew* — a fully-fleshed narrative told in 356 words — a daughter copes with her mother's mental illness by retreating into the adventures of Nancy Drew, a place that offers her a greater sense of control; a world where the people she loves might still be saved.

Joshua Goudie's second-place winner, *Satsuma and Cigarettes*, introduces readers to a father struggling to be the best parent he can be, but whose illegal pursuits inevitably lead to the loss of his daughter.

Third-place winner *Bliss*, by Janet Kelly, depicts one of the most painful periods in a young woman's life, as she makes the transition between childhood and adulthood — a journey that is rarely without incident and often involves a loss of innocence.

Another motif is the notion of home, and yes, it truly is where the heart is and it's often the place where hearts are broken, when relationships end or loved ones die, jolting our emotional foundations.

In Amanda Stephen's *Coming Home*, an addict sees home as both safe haven and land of temptation; a place where there is love and support, but where is there also a familiarity that could mean her undoing.

"When everyone knows who you are," the protagonist muses, "there's no escaping your former self. There are no masks in outports, and maybe that's what I love and hate about it all."

In Elizabeth Wright's *Home*, a sister berates her brother for being a "professional Newfoundlander," but comes to realize there is nothing hypocritical or false about finding security in a sense of place and tradition.

In Annette Conway's poignant *Unloving You*, a couple's sense of home is shattered as the space between them grows and threatens to become a chasm.

"They don't speak to each other as they drive out Torbay Road unless it is to tell the other about something one of the boys said or did. It's all they have between them anymore."

It's not all love and loss, of course. There are dystopian stories here, too — glimpses of a future you might well be glad to avoid. And there's humour — black, nasty, murderous humour.

Consider Dolores Hynes' *Killing with Kindness*: "I thought about mixing a bit of anti-freeze with his drink, or shoving him down the cellar stairs when he was half in the bag (just to hurry things along) but the risk of getting caught wasn't worth it. A scattered time I'd be overcome with guilt, but then I'd see the smug look on ol' Saucy Puss as I lugged in boughs for the fire and all feelings of remorse would vanish."

I hope readers enjoy each one of these stories and their sometimes familiar settings, from the parking lot of a closed gas station in Stephenville to a seat on a Metrobus on LeMarchant Road in

St. John's. This collection represents the rich writing talent of this province.

And should *Cuffer Anthology: Volume V* whet your appetite for *Volumes I, II, III and IV*, you should know that proceeds from the sale of these books go to a good cause — Literacy Newfoundland and Labrador.

The writers whose work is represented here are either well known or they should be. May you enjoy the fruits of their fertile imaginations as much as I have, as have our Cuffer Prize judges, Ramona Dearing, Joan Sullivan and Russell Wangersky.

Thanks to them, and special thanks to Todd Manning and Joanne Snook-Hann for the wonderful layout, Donna Francis and Pam Dooley of Creative Book Publishing for their unflagging enthusiasm, and to my husband, Glenn Payette, for his support and encouragement.

Pam Frampton
St. John's

Nancy Drew

By Wanda Nolan

1st-place winner of the Cuffer Prize 2012

Nancy Drew lived in the densely packed gift shop at St. Clare's Hospital. The yellow books sat on the bottom row of the bookcase in the back, surrounded by fluorescent lights, neon "Get Better Soon" balloons and white bears strangled with red ribbons. A miniature picture of a blond girl holding a spyglass adorned the side of each spine. I got to choose a book each visit, a thank you for accompanying my mother on her monthly psychiatric appointments.

At first the books were used to avoid the heavy eyes of the other patients that sat along the narrow waiting area to see Dr. Spencer. Depression a halo over each person's head. The nurse would open the door and announce down the long aisle the next person to enter the smaller waiting area inside. When it was time, my mother would sidle her way down the hallway until she slipped through the door at the end. I imagined her moving from smaller room to smaller room until she was squeezed into a tiny confessional chamber where the doctor, hunched like a king crab, whispered advice. I decided to call it, The Mystery of the Secret Room.

There was one patient named Randall who was on the same schedule as my mother. He had a long neck and his head drooped around it like a crane. He wore a navy jacket with Esso written across the front where his heart would be. After my mother would go into the doctor's office, he would move across the room and sit next to me. You see, he hated to see anyone alone. I pushed further into the world on the page, entering my own chamber — one much happier than what I imagined for my mother — the town of River Heights. There, Nancy leaned in, looked close: two clips to hold a heavy bang, eyeglasses with the wrong prescription, a broken shell. All clues pieced together like a torn up letter from the past. The telegraphed message an inevitable danger that Nancy figured out just in time to save her boyfriend Ned, her best friend Bess, her mom and dad.

• • •

WANDA NOLAN *writes fiction and screenplays. Her work has appeared in various anthologies and journals, including Riddle Fence. In 2009, she won the Newfoundland and Labrador Arts & Letters Award for her short film script "Four Sisters." The short has run a successful film festival circuit and the feature is in development with Odd Sock Productions. In 2012, she also won the Atlantic Film Festival's Inspired Script Award for her feature film "The Magic of Boxer Connors." Currently, she is working on a novel called "Rabbittown." Nolan grew up in Freshwater, Placentia Bay, and lives in St. John's. In May 2013, she won the CBC Emerging Artist Award from the Newfoundland and Labrador Arts Council.*

Satsuma and Cigarettes

By Joshua Goudie

2nd-place winner of the Cuffer Prize 2012

I picked the little bits of dirt and rock out from under the torn skin before raising my knuckles to my mouth. My tongue flicked over the fresh wound, chasing that hard iron flavour. I had grown accustomed to it, but it was usually from sniffing nosebleeds into the back of my throat. Hot showers in the morning mixed with damaged sinuses have a way of bringing those on.

They didn't seem all that interested in me; I guess because I was already on the ground and they could see I wasn't going anywhere. I sat up and looked at the darkening sky as ribbons of red and blue light swirled above me. There was a second where everything went quiet and I closed my eyes and it was like I could feel the lights washing my skin. It was actually quite calming.

Then it all broke. "Don't you dare move," someone said. Maybe the officer who pulled me out of the car? I don't know. They all sound the same, don't they? "Where is it?"

It was tucked up into a hollowed out space in the headrest. A little better than right there in the ashtray, but not much. I knew they'd be finding it soon enough.

"I said don't move!"

That's when the hard knee jutted into my spine, collapsing my body forward, face first onto the flaking blacktop. I suppose I shouldn't have done it but I took another chance and shifted to get a look at my watch. She would be arriving at the house right about now. I told her I might not be home when she got there but she knew where I kept the extra key. It's hard trying to find a spot to hide a spare key on Long's Hill but I've become pretty resourceful over the years. Not that the present moment showed any of that.

"Come on. Where is it?"

This was to be her first night staying over in months. The last time there'd been a racket over what I thought was an appropriate meal. It can be the littlest things sometimes.

"Where!?"

But after much discussion and too many phone calls she was coming back. But tonight she would be coming back to an empty home with no explanations. At least not yet. Explanations would be coming soon though, I knew that.

She would need to get a shower first thing when she arrived, she'd told me when she phoned last night. I always love the way the house smells when she stays over. Especially after a shower. Satsuma and cigarettes. That's me and her in a nutshell. Her goodness always trying to beat back my bad.

She'd be coming over straight after her dance class. She'd been taking classes down on Queen's Road and said that tonight she was going to teach me. "Just for fun," she said. I had cleared the coffee table out of the living room and pushed the TV up against the wall earlier that day so she'd have the room. I wasn't all that keen on learning but this would be the first time I'd have seen her in over a month so I would have let her teach me to be a snake charmer if she wanted to.

"Can you explain this?" came another voice. With my face in the pavement, inches from the gasoline rainbow puddles, I couldn't see what they were talking about but I had a feeling. A car door, which I guessed was mine, slammed and I knew their hunt was over.

I wasn't sure if I was supposed to cook for us again so I'd gone to the grocery store just to be safe. I bought a package of pre-made cheese tortellini and a Greek salad. I knew she hated olives so I'd already gone through and picked them off the top. Pasta and salad. There would be no complaints from anyone this time.

"No explanation?"

How long would she just wait around, I wondered. I was having nightmarish visions of her searching through the kitchen cupboards, looking for the phonebook so she could call the office. "I'm sorry, but he no longer holds a position here."

"All right," I heard someone say, then my arms were wrenched behind my back and I felt the unkind bite of the cold, metal bracelets. "Time to go."

They hoisted me up, grabbing me by arms, and began leading me towards their SUV. On the way I took a look up into the sky, realizing this might be one of my last chances to breathe fresh summer air for awhile. Above me I could only make out a single star shining through the fog.

This was supposed to be my second chance. Now my last second chance, more than likely. How could she be a part of my life after all this gets out?

I'll be spending my night in the lockup now and she'll be alone in the house. And it will soon be past her bedtime.

I'd always tried to be perfect for her. I always wanted to be the kind of dad any little girl would want. And deserve. But I'm like a stuffed animal, filled with broken glass. I guess this is the day she finds out.

JOSHUA ALEXANDER GOUDIE was born in Grand Falls-Windsor. In 2007 he graduated from Sir Wilfred Grenfell College with a bachelor's degree in fine arts. He is working on his first novel.

Bliss

By Janet Kelly

3rd-place winner of the Cuffer Prize 2012

One o'clock. A weekday. The middle of summer. I'm in the kitchen, surrounded by papers and books and I don't have a job. I've been reading and writing and philosophizing the way a girl from around the bay only gets to do once in her life, in the July after her first year of university. After going away and moving back home again for the very first time, alone.

Now Dad is standing in the triangle of light created by the open door and the inside of the nearly empty fridge. He is looking for something and I know what it is. It is a ham sandwich on white baker's bread that he made last night and placed on the top shelf, next to a bottle of beets.

Here is my father on his lunch break in his short-sleeved shirt and grey dress pants, forehead on the freezer door, bent at the waist. The brown and purple striped tie hanging from his throat moves in a slight circular motion, reminding me of a wedding band suspended on a piece of thread, like the one that old Mrs. Penney across the street has been using for years to determine the sex of God knows how many fetuses inside God knows how many giddy expectant mothers, fat in their silly floral blouses and elastic-waisted polyester hand-me-down pants.

And here I am, ready to answer his question.

"Did you see that sandwich?"

I look at him blankly from my regular seat at the head of the table. My face flushes and pales the way it does when I lie through my teeth. It wonders me how he does not notice this, after 18 years.

Which sandwich?

"A ham sandwich. I made two last night and ate one before bed. Was Uncle Fin or anyone here earlier for lunch?"

Nope. Haven't seen Uncle Fin all week.

Dad moves the bottle of beets. Moves the Fluffo shortening, the blue 2-litre of milk, the block of Old Fort cheese. Opens the drawer with the carrots and then the one with the onions. I see his breath, just for a second, when he tries inside the freezer.

"Did you eat it?" He turns and looks directly at me, right in my eyes. The light from inside the harvest gold fridge is like a halo behind him, or a fire.

No! I'm a vegetarian, remember? Vehement because I need him to think that he is out of touch. Because he is.

A sigh. He can't understand what happened to it, then. He pours himself a glass of milk and sits across from me at the table. I look down. I need him to go away.

Do you want me to get you something else?

"Yes, please. If you don't mind."

I make him one tuna sandwich with Miracle Whip and one with relish. He eats them both without a word, chugs another glass of milk, and retires to the bathroom with an Export 'A' and a copy of Columbia. The only place he gets any privacy, I guess. The Knights of Columbus the only club he ever joined that still sends a free magazine every month, regardless of whether he pays his dues or not.

I know that Dad is done in the bathroom when I smell the combination of cigarette smoke, toothpaste and shit emanating from the hallway. I will be smothered and sickened by this; it will linger in my nostrils throughout the remainder of my pregnancy. Luckily, my appointment is on the 30th. I'll finally be rid of it and with it the nausea and the heightened sense of smell. Not to mention the insatiable cravings for cured and vacuum-sealed luncheon meats.

"It's a queer thing happened to that sandwich," Dad says when he enters the kitchen again. He opens the fridge door once more. I'm soon going to vomit and give myself away.

"Unless … unless Uncle Fin was here while I was in the shower or something. Earlier."

"Must have been, I s'pose. Yes, that must be it."

He is satisfied. He slips his shoes back on and says he'll see me after work. I should have supper ready, as usual.

I give him a peck on the cheek and then I go to the window to watch and make sure that he has walked down through the garden and out of sight before I dare curl up in the swivel rocker to cry. For all the things I can't tell him. All the things my father doesn't know.

...

JANET KELLY is a multitasker and positive thinker living somewhere between the truth and a lie on the Northeast Avalon. When not writing or telling stories, she likes to daydream and walk alongside the ocean.

Two-Man Tent

By Robert Chafe

Cuffer Prize 2012 Honourable Mention

When I was 17 my father and I finally went camping. It was August and I was in my last month before the big move to Halifax for school. The weather had been unusually fine, thick days of sunlight and warm nights, and my father surprised us all one day by venturing into the far reaches of the garage and emerging with a long forgotten two-man tent. I didn't doubt his good intentions, but readied myself for disappointment. He had been, for the majority of my life, a man heavily devoted to his work. That his family rarely saw him was of little import as long as there was stability and shelter. "Your father is a provider," my mother told me. She would often apologize for him in the form of a compliment.

My father booked off a long weekend at his busiest time of year and bought a provincial map at the gas station at the foot of our street. He seemed to take some pleasure in planning the entire trip before leaving town, everything broken down and noted on the map to the very minute and mile. We left St. John's early on a Thursday morning, the back seat full, and a rented and fully loaded trailer behind us to demonstrate his commitment. We were headed for Sand Banks Provincial Park, tucked into the furthest corner of the island down near Burgeo, where Dad said even good weather wouldn't draw crowds. He never did like people very much, at least not in substantial numbers. I watched him driving, waited for him to change his mind, to remember something more important and temporarily forgotten. He never looked at me, and he never broke 90 kilometres an hour. My mother had told him to take his time.

We had driven this road before, countless times, when I was younger and there was more time. Me, my father and my mother, making the 12-hour drive from St. John's to St. Anthony to visit her sister. Clarenville in the bay at the base of the hills, Gander stretching next to the lake, the great sweep of the road up and overlooking Glovertown. Grand Falls where the highway sliced fast and hard through the centre. Stretches of road in between with a long history of silence and then slowly tourist booths and craft stores, camping lodges, hotels and restaurants now, chains with commercials on TV. But this was a road into nothing once.

He had believed and declared firmly that there was a gas station just outside the western limits of Corner Brook and when one didn't present itself before the turnoff to Burgeo his plans hit a hard wall. The road we were to travel was a long one, a three-hour exit route with a sign posted at its entrance: No gas for 350 kilometres. Dad eyed the gauge and cursed under his breath, rolled the car around and headed back toward the exit into Bay St. George. We were going to Stephenville in the hunt for fuel.

My father hated Stephenville, and had called it the arsehole of Newfoundland when his finger had grazed it on the map. When we found our first gas station it was dark, empty and un-helpful. There was a flipped "Closed" sign and the doors were locked. "It's four o'clock on Thursday afternoon. People need gas." It was the most he'd said in hours.

In the distance an electrical storm clicked its way across the top of the bay. The sky out towards St. George's looked as though night had come early with some serious flashes of warning. In the spreading gloom the town of Stephenville was growing blurry for lack of light. A sub-routing station at the top of the bay had been hit, taking out power to the entire peninsula. Every gas station and amenity within a hundred kilometres lay dormant, and their idle employees planted themselves at their front doors smoking and delivering the bad news: they were not expecting power to be back up and running for hours. We drove around and around but our impatience changed nothing.

We sat in the car then, myself and my father, in the parking lot of a closed café. There was a sad kind of silence as he looked again at the map and tried to discern how it had failed him. I suggested waiting for the power to come back, and then continuing on our way down to the park.

"Your mother doesn't want us driving at night."

"We don't have to tell her."

He folded the map and put it for the first time in the glove compartment. He sneezed then and apologized instead of excusing himself, and drove us down the road to the Stephenville Holiday Inn. At the front desk, lit by dim reserve power, he looked for too long in his wallet, and told me that he was very tired from it all, the driving. He booked us each a separate room. My father said he'd meet me for breakfast at eight, and that having lost a night we'd best just head back home after that. "Fucking town," he grumbled as he was walking away.

The hotel was clean, but the bed was hard. I lay there watching the storm move off in the distance, and the darkness land for real. Around nine o'clock the power came on, and with it the television. I watched the news, and a story about a family killed on the 401 in Ontario and I wanted to call my mother. I knew if I did I would awaken a worry in her, so I closed my eyes and let the impulse pass. I was about to move away from home for the first time, charge fully into freedom and I had no idea of what to expect. I wanted someone to tell me.

In the whirr of the outdated air conditioner I thought I heard my father's voice, distant and low behind the walls, and through my closed eyes I saw his face again as we drove around Stephenville looking for gas. There had been an inexplicable fire in him then, given life and breath for the first time in years. His eyes were wide and his mouth was pulled into a fierce tight line. At the time I was sure it was anger or frustration. But now with age and distance, I can't shake for a second that his look was one more of relief.

...

ROBERT CHAFE *is a St. John's-based writer whose work as a playwright has been seen across Canada, the U.K., Australia and in the States. He was shortlisted for the Governor General's Award for Drama ("Tempting Providence" and "Butler's Marsh") in 2004, and won the award for "Afterimage" in 2010.*

Unloving You

By Annette Conway

Cuffer Prize 2012 Honourable Mention

He knows exactly when they broke. He can almost tell you the precise time, right down to the minute, and he thinks she knows it too but she won't admit it. At least not yet. Not until it gets worse than it is. Though he can't imagine that's possible. Yet it is. And it does.

He moves her hair off her shoulders before he zips her up and then lays it back as it was. He used to tell her she was lovely but he can't bring himself to do it tonight. It's not that she isn't beautiful. She is. It's just that he doesn't care enough to even say it anymore. They kiss the boys goodnight and tell them that they won't be late and to listen to the sitter and to go to bed on time.

They don't speak to each other as they drive out Torbay Road unless it is to tell the other about something one of the boys said or did. It's all they have between them anymore. They stop at the lights at Stavanger Drive and he recalls how he drove around the subdivision there last week after work and before he went home and looked at the houses with "For Sale" signs on them. He had slowed down in front of those houses to catch a glimpse of the people inside and wondered what he would look like in their place. What the boys would be like living on this street. With him. Without her.

Raymonds is full and they are shown to their table where Chris and Jennifer are already seated. They shake hands and kiss and place their orders and raise their wine in a toast. It is an ordinary night of ordinary people. His leg is resting against Jennifer's and he feels the heat of her through his pants and he wonders if she feels it too. She doesn't move her leg and his mind wanders and he ponders the unthinkable, the undoable. He tries to imagine it and he finds himself enjoying it.

His wife is funny tonight. She has captured their attention with her stories and regaled them with anecdotes that have them laughing. He remembers that this is the way she was when they first met and that this was one of the things he had found attractive in her. The right balance of humour and sensitivity, spontaneity and sensibility. He watches and listens and in his objectivity he realizes she is the same person she ever was. Except to the extent that they have ruined each other.

She asked him the other day what it was that he wanted from her. What could she do to make this work. He tried to keep his voice from escalating into that high pitch that signals a fight is about to come, but it's hard to do. It's hard to be restrained when you just want to scream the truth. He had wanted to say I want to unmeet you, I want to unknow you, I want to unlove you. I want to go back in time and to have never said hello to you. I want to know then what I know now. I want the opportunity to have made a better choice. But he had said nothing. I want nothing from you.

They walk down Water Street and onto the waterfront and Jennifer and Chris are holding hands. He feels he should take her hand but it is an effort just for the thought let alone the action and so he doesn't. He puts his hands in his pockets and holds the crumpled tissues that he finds instead. Jennifer is talking about her mother who has recently died and he recalls being at the funeral home and looking at the photographs of the deceased on the wall and the picture of her mother and father together when they were young and so obviously in love that it was physically painful to look at them. He had felt like he was intruding on a private moment just by looking at that picture and it hurt him to see it because you just knew they were two people who didn't know who they were without each other.

They say goodnight and get into their cars to drive back to their respective lives. The ride home is mostly silent and punctuated only by the odd comment about the evening and then she startles him when she asks if he thinks Chris and Jennifer are happy. He doesn't know what to say to that because he doesn't even know what it means and so he says nothing and they resume their silence.

He remembers the day they got the call from the doctor after the tests and how she had wanted her to come in as soon as possible. How they couldn't talk to each other and how he couldn't look at her just to see his fear mirrored in her eyes and how they had played with the kids in the snow but forgot to build a snowman and just shovelled the same snow from one place to another. How they both breathed a collective sigh of relief and how his voice broke on the phone when she said everything was fine. He wants to love her that much again. To have his voice betray him for the love that was in it.

They brush their teeth next to each other and she finishes first and goes to their room. He looks in the mirror and looks himself in the eye and wonders if he could do it. Could he have an affair. Could he cheat on her even with all of this and all of nothing between them. Could he go through with it. It is appealing and exciting and he longs to feel something for someone again. He looks at his face in the mirror once more and knows he couldn't. He does not want to be that kind of man. He does not ever want to have to tell his children that he is that kind of man.

The lights are out in their room and he feels his way to the bed along the familiar path he has taken for the last 13 years. He once read that after a bone breaks and knits back together, it is actually stronger in the area of the break than it was before. Maybe it's a myth. Maybe it's the truth. Either way it's a risk he'll take. She is on her own side of the bed facing the wall and he slides across the sheets and spoons into her back and wraps his arms around her for whatever comfort there is in it.

∙∙∙

ANNETTE CONWAY *was born in St. John's. After studying law in Ontario she returned to St. John's where she now practises. She lives in Torbay with her partner and their two children and is at work on her first novel. She has been shortlisted four times for the Cuffer Prize.*

Being Frank

BY RANDY DROVER

Cuffer Prize 2012 Honourable Mention

Frank is bundled like the dead, and has been talking incessantly since we left Georgetown. He goes on and on, following the circular path of a true hypochondriac. Back to the foot arches and the urine tests. Frank didn't have back pain or kidney trouble, but death was in every cell of his body.

There's a smell of tar coming off the road. It's freshly paved, so we cut down the waterfront to avoid car tires spitting asphalt chewing-gum in our direction.

Frank is convinced that the streets are lurking with danger. He marvels at men walking in and out of dark alleys. Frank clings to the curb, avoiding cars and overhanging signs. He's always fearful of the old brick buildings in the downtown core. Brick is the first thing to go, he says. If you had a good steel building it would withstand a quake.

Newfoundland hasn't had an earthquake in 80 years, I tell him.

I wait outside the clinic and light a cigarette. It's unusually hot and all the windows in the clinic are cracked an inch. There's a little red bench just outside the clinic that I sit on, back against the front wall. Frank brings me out the paper to read. The clinic always has the paper. I get through the first couple of pages each day. The important things are always in front.

The old women inside are talking. Frank doesn't have strong ears and they all know it. The waiting room has turned into a support group for the ill; for Frank. He rambles about the tormented struggle he's having with his back these days. Can't piss without sitting down. Most of them know Frank and they pity him. Pity is worse than any narcotic, it's far more addictive.

Bernice leaves the clinic. She's wearing her heels again, walking like a newborn calf. A younger man holds the door open for her. I recognize him from the mini mart and I nod. He lifts a bag of frozen Asian stir-fry mix to his face and goes inside. He tells the group what happened. This young missus, he says, wanted to get in the shop for a tub of milk. I told her it'd be quicker to milk her cat, cause she ain't gettin' in here till I finishes my smoke, he says.

Broke his nose, this girl. I figure it's the right thing, too. But nobody inside says that. They all tell him it'll be OK, that it makes him look tougher.

Frank's name is called, and I toss my cigarette and fold the paper under my arm. I walk around the back of the building and find the doctor's open window.

Frank looks slightly uplifted when he comes out of the clinic. He'd taken his sweater off anyway. Most days, when he was home, Frank paraded about in Daisy Dukes. Shorts cut far too high, and with uneven pieces of white cotton hanging down from being cut with the kitchen scissors. When he steps foot outside, even in the heat, he wears at least three layers.

I think I might need an operation, Frank says.

I have to get to work, I say.

• • •

Beneath the girders of the warehouse, I work on getting some motor oil ready to ship. One of the bottles in the box is broken and I try to wash the oil off the rest of them. The smell makes me gag, and reminds me of Frank's hair, combed out with thick teeth and grease. Frank makes me sick sometimes. He gives off a faint, greenish steam of decay. I imagine he glows in the dark.

I'm more like Frank than I care to admit. I like to think I'm not as bad, but there's a reason I put up with his madness, help him out on occasion, walk him to the clinic.

Little things bug him. Punishment from God, he believes. A broken hook on a screen, batteries running out, light switch broken, mattress too soft, too hard, not as springy as it was when he first bought it.

I have quirks, too. But God had nothing to do with them. I eat oranges at an alarming pace. Always have enough to get me through another day, like smokes. I thought I remembered some rhyme about oranges and mental heath, like apples and the doctor, but maybe I imagined it. I get little headaches sometimes, and I shake my head so fast that the people around me turn into blurred grey ghosts.

I sensed a connection with Frank when he first came here. Frank always did most of the talking, but when I spoke, Frank listened completely. When he talked, I did the same.

I guess I wanted to believe that if I could be happy for Frank it would mean that I was happy, like when you see a couple holding hands. On good days you're happy for them.

•••

Frank calls. He lives downstairs, but he always calls. Going to run down to the doctor, he says. Meet you out front?

Sure thing Frank, I say. I tell the dog to go lay down.

I try the doorknob and hear the pin snap inside. A quiet nose, like the low tick just before the alarm clock starts. The knob spins in circles. Each time it spins I feel it catch for just a second before letting go. I start to chuckle. A low guttural tremor before the quake.

I hear Frank outside calling me. He sees the handle spinning, and comes over to see if he can jimmy it open. I hate when things like this happen, he says.

Your full of shit, Frank, I say, voice rising to a crackle, aggravated at the doorknob. I hip-check the door. The steel door. You're not sick, Frank! You're 35 and you dress like you're 70! You're healthy as a horse. I know that's what the doctor tells you! We're not going to the goddamn doctor. You're not sitting in a room with a dozen old hens telling you it'll be fine and patting your head. We're taking the car today, Frank, and we're not going to crash. We're going to the hardware store and I'm buying a new knob. And we're taking the dog.

I rest my head on the door, palms on the doorbox. There's silence for a full minute.

I'm coming around, I say. Down through the fire escape.

I'll grab some cash, he says. I need some light bulbs.

•••

There were delays from the paving crew, and the traffic was backed up past the Brass Rack. Frank was wearing cargo shorts.

I heard the dog bark after a couple of minutes.

•••

RANDY DROVER *is an award-winning writer living in St. John's. He works in publishing and edits poetry at Riddle Fence.*

Judy McDermid's Garden of Faeries

By Jamie Fitzpatrick

Cuffer Prize 2012 Honourable Mention

The first one arrived right before her eyes.

She was in the sunroom, deadheading the begonia, when it tumbled from the sky like a bird with a broken wing, bouncing off a flagstone and skidding to a halt in the long grass. Judy watched as it struggled to get airborne again. But its ugly brown wings were soaking wet, and at least one leg appeared to be bent the wrong way.

When it stopped flailing, Judy saw that the creature had her brother's face. Not life-sized, but a face that suited the body, about the size of a fist. Judy hadn't seen her brother since the racket over the money. She had stopped speaking to him after that, and he died quite suddenly before they had a chance to reconcile.

She called his name, but the creature didn't answer.

The second one must have walked from somewhere, because its wings were damaged beyond repair. It was more interesting to look at, with a fuzzy green body like a caterpillar. It staggered about the garden, restless and apparently in pain.

Judy followed at a distance, and when she got a good look she saw the face of the first boy she ever had sex with, the summer after Grade 11. Her friend Martha had said she would live to regret that night. Martha was wrong. The act itself was something of a disaster — Judy should have given the poor guy some advance warning — but once she lost her virginity she understood what a worthless commodity it had been. So she always had a soft spot for the boy. He was dead now, too.

The third one was hateful. Judy shooed it away with a broom, then watched it return and perch atop the shed, all high and mighty. It was lovely, coloured like a monarch butterfly. But in the face Judy saw that batty English professor, the one who dressed like a slut and gave her a failing grade in romantic poetry. Romantic poetry was a required course, so failure was quite a blow. She went into a tailspin for about six months after that.

For three days this monster strutted about the garden, flipping its hair and wiggling its bottom. On the fourth morning Judy opened the door and threw a heavy glass ashtray at it. Pretty good shot, clipped a wing and sent the thing into spasms of pain.

The sense of triumph was like nothing she had felt in years.

The fourth one touched down a week later. It was small and grey, and fat like a moth. The face was that of a little boy who had played with Elizabeth on summer days. Judy remembered them always running, across lawns, between houses, down the street to the playground. Watching the fat faerie skip over wet grass, Judy could scarcely believe her luck, how happy she had been back then. But she hadn't known the boy's family very well. She couldn't recall his name. Why had he appeared?

Maybe she was dying. Odd that faeries — if that's what they were — would keep turning up in her yard, bearing faces from her past. Could she be having a stroke or aneurism? Maybe only a few seconds had passed since the day she had been deadheading the begonia, and she was still there, collapsed over the plant, hallucinating as life slipped away.

The fifth one left her heartsick. It was long and slender, and shimmered metallic blue. She knew before she saw the face. It was that awful, beautiful man from human resources.

Everyone assumes a woman will choose a dull, workaday fellow for marriage and save the hard case for her affair. But it had been quite the opposite with Judy. Neil was always a bit of a wild man, even after they were married and the kids were born. The guy from human resources was the quiet one. They used to sit together without talking, or even moving. That's how Judy remembered him.

She understood this creature, the way it looked sadly about the garden, hovering in the air and touching lightly on tree branches. Its long antennae moved with grace and purpose, like a matching set of conductor's batons.

The sixth one convinced Judy to seek help. It didn't look like anyone she had ever known, but after several days she recognized the face. It was a minor actress from the movie she had watched the night after Neil passed away. A stupid movie about aliens who invade Earth and suck everyone's guts out. She had just sat there on the couch and watched it, relieved to have a few hours to herself, a few hours away from Neil's hysterical family.

Judy called Elizabeth and told her everything. Elizabeth listened without interrupting, then asked, "Are you sure they're faeries, Mom?" Judy said she didn't know what they were. Elizabeth suggested she call the MUN Folklore Department. "They know all about faeries over there."

The seventh one was awful, spitting and snarling and making guttural noises that sounded like curse words. It abused itself, flying into walls and fence posts, climbing into the grey sky to make hurtling kamikaze runs into trees and shrubbery. Once it crashed into the picnic table with a crack so loud Judy heard it through the kitchen window. It could only be her father. But he looked so young, the way he must have looked long before Judy was born.

The eighth one was her mother, black and feathery and haggard.

Dreading the battle that was sure to erupt between her parents, Judy finally called the Folklore Department. After explaining her situation to a receptionist, she was handed off to a man who sounded too young to be an expert in anything.

"It doesn't sound like any faerie story I've ever heard," he said. She asked if he might come and take them away, but this wasn't possible.

Judy was scared. She wasn't sure she could live in the house anymore.

The man asked what she was scared of.

"I'm afraid I might be dying," said Judy.

The man paused. Then he said, "We're all dying, Mrs. McDermid."

•••

JAMIE FITZPATRICK'S *debut novel, "You Could Believe in Nothing" (Vagrant Press), is a winner of the Fresh Fish Award for Emerging Writers from the Literary Arts Foundation of Newfoundland and Labrador. He is a freelance writer and broadcaster, and an online columnist for the About.com network.*

✓Foreshore

By Joshua Goudie

Cuffer Prize 2012 Honourable Mention

I had no idea how old she was. Not until they dragged us both up off the frozen beach rocks and threw us into the back of the cruiser. We must have looked quite the pair.

"Is this your son?" they'd asked her. Son. Who in their right mind would get into that sort of situation with their son? Idiots.

The first time I laid eyes to her was when me and Gossey stormed through the well-worn front door of the bar and marched up to the counter like this was something we had done a thousand times before. She laughed before we even had ourselves parked on a stool.

"How old are you?" she asked.

"Nineteen," we lied.

She wasn't having any of that though. "How old?"

"Well missus," Gossey replied honestly, "if I sees another year I'll be 15."

She laughed again at that then told us to get lost. She wasn't mean about it. In fact, she smiled at us the whole time. I guess that's why we felt safe trying our luck again a week later.

She'd let us drink in the stock room. We'd walk in the front door, she'd tell us to go home out of it, then two minutes later she'd show up at the back door to let us in. For 20 bucks she'd sell us a bottle of whatever she had that was more or less full. And we always had enough for a bottle on account of Gossey selling his grandfather's pain pills around school.

Mostly we'd just sit on the floor and play cards. We'd start off playing Texas Hold'em, but as the night wore on and the two of us got sillier we'd fall back into more childish games like Go Fish or Crazy Eights. That's how she usually found us when she'd come back to check up on us; roaring drunk in the middle of a game of Fish.

One night she sold us a bottle of this awful, red, sour stuff. We managed to stomach most of it down but Gossey ended up getting sick to his guts and throwing up all over the place. When she came back to see what we were up to Gossey was passed out in the corner and I was on my knees wiping up his mess with a roll of shop towels. She looked us over and shook her head. "Youngsters."

Gossey ended up leaving to go air himself out before heading home while I stayed to finish the cleanup job. I was just getting ready to head out myself when she came back again. "Another day, another dollar," she said as she looked around the room. It still stank of the poisonous stomach bile but at least it looked clean. She nodded her head approvingly before slumping into the wall. Even in my condition I could tell that she was in a bit of a similar state herself.

"Come on out front," she said. "I've still got to clean up before we can go."

We, I thought to myself. I didn't know where exactly it was that we were going but it was just the two of us now. I'd have followed her anywhere and I think she knew it.

After she locked up she took me by the hand and walked me down along the beach. Her hands were still sticky from the blue spray cleaner she used to wipe down the bar; it was like her skin was biting into mine. I loved it.

We listened to the rolling ocean as we slipped along the smooth skin of the beach rocks. We had to hold on tight to keep from going down. We both laughed as we stumbled and jerked each other around for support.

I remember as soon as I saw the boat knocking against the rocks thinking, How easy would it be to steal that? It was only a weak little dory but badness was something my mind always went to first. Apparently so did hers because while my next few thoughts were of all the reasons I should just leave the thing alone, she shook off my hand and went down and climbed aboard. "How's about a ride?" she asked. That was all the convincing I needed to get out my knife and start savagely cutting through the hard, green rope.

She made me row. I did my best to sit up straight and dig the oars in deep, showing off how fast I could get us going. She sat across from me, relaxed and splayed out like a cat. It was as if she was at home, comfortably on her couch and not trapped out on the water being carted around by some mad drunken teenager.

She leaned forward at one point to tie the laces of my boot. I hadn't even noticed that they'd come undone but in that moment it was like my entire body shut down and the only part that remained alert was my foot. She was so gentle.

It couldn't have been too long after that when we went over. I don't know how. Maybe we run up against something or maybe one of us leaned the wrong way, but regardless, we went over and then under. And all I was thinking was, we're gonna end up on the news.

But we never did. We both managed our way back to shore, calling for our breath and stinking of salt water.

And that was the first time I saw her. I mean really saw her. Her clothes were sticking to her like a second skin and I lay on my side making out her shape. She wasn't thin. She had wide curves that swelled and collapsed against the moonlight but I didn't care. I just wanted to look.

That's when the cops showed up. The owner of the boat had looked out his window, seen his property missing and called it in. "Probably just a couple of kids," they'd told him.

I only saw her once more after that. Gossey and me were playing street hockey a few weeks later when I noticed someone watching us from a car. Sure enough it was herself.

When I got over there I crouched down to her window and asked where she was headed. "I've got to start repenting," she said. "I think my sins have battered my soul." I don't know what she meant by that but I noticed she had a fat lip and a missing tooth when she spoke.

A few nights after that we were down on the beach when Gossey announced he had swiped a bottle of liquor off his parents. I was eager as he reached into his jacket but he ended up pulling out a flask of that awful red stuff. He said he had only taken it for a laugh and had plans on putting it back but we ended up coming across the same pathetic little dory from my night out. We poured the booze all over it then burned her to ashes.

•••

JOSHUA ALEXANDER GOUDIE was born in Grand Falls-Windsor. In 2007 he graduated from Sir Wilfred Grenfell College with a bachelor's degree in fine arts. He is working on his first novel.

Slideshow

By Dara Squires

Cuffer Prize 2012 Honourable Mention

Aunt Lou showed up unannounced at suppertime on Sunday: pork roast with applesauce and boiled potatoes. There's never enough applesauce. But with Aunt Lou showing up unexpected there was even less. I don't know why Mom doesn't just make double. It's not like it'll go bad.

After supper, Mom was in the kitchen, stewing, judging by the clatter of dishes. She wanted me to join in loudly bashing the plates into the drain rack and quietly criticizing her sister, but Aunt Lou drew me in like the sound of milk hitting a saucer calls the cats.

She has a trunk: a real trunk, like the one up in the attic that Dad's great-grandmother brought over on the boat from Ireland. But our ancestor never had anything near what Lou has in her trunk: three hats — in hatboxes! And 10 pairs of shoes, including one pair of winter boots that have spiky heels that would be about as good in the snow as nails in sand.

No one around here wears hats or high-heeled boots or silky scarves from India. I'm lucky if Mom remembers to take off her apron and do her hair when they're playing cards. She worries more about getting the dip in a perfect mound on the platter and the cocktail weenies and onions straight on the toothpicks than she does about looking good herself.

Aunt Lou is different. Maybe it's because she's the youngest; maybe she just isn't old enough yet to be stodgy and worried about ironed sheets. But I have a feeling that even when she's as old as Mom is she won't be like her.

Except for a couple of my uncles who moved off for work, the furthest anyone in the family ever went was to move from Grand Falls to St. John's. But Lou, Lou went straight to Montreal when she wasn't much older than I am now. Aunt Norma went too, to join the Sisters of the Holy Cross. But you always get the feeling that Lou went and Norma tagged along, even though Norma was older.

One time, I saw a picture of Lou in a swimsuit at my friend's house. She even autographed it. My friend's dad went to a car show in Toronto where she was modelling. He couldn't have been prouder when he realized she was from Newfoundland and there as a real model. "You couldn't smack the smile off my face," he said, "when she opened her mouth to say hello, I knew before the 'oh' was out that she were from Grand Falls!"

That was right before she married Roberto. She was only 19 and he was her photographer. They lived all over the world. That's about all I know. No one tells me much. I know she left him. But I'm not supposed to talk about it. Roberto beat Aunt Lou up. She called Mom, sobbing, and then next thing anyone knows Aunt Norma has flown to Mexico and is dragging Lou home with her.

I was just a kid then. Aunt Lou had bruises all over her face and when I asked about it near everyone in the room told me to shush. But Aunt Norma pulled me away and explained that some men thought they owned women and could hit them.

"Did a man ever own you?" I asked, which was foolish considering she's a nun. But how'd she know so much about it, I was wondering.

That's when she told me to shush, too.

Norma went to a special convent in Montreal, maybe that's why she seems different to the nuns here. I suppose she had a calling, though she doesn't seem that type. Lou heard the world calling, she says. It got so loud in her ears that she had to walk toward it so it would stop shouting.

Lou took everything that was in her closet when she left, including all her modelling clothes — and her wedding dress. She's kept it all this time and takes it everywhere in the bottom of her trunk.

That dress is why she and I are standing in the shivering fog at Cape Spear, by the cannons, so I can take her photo.

"Don't ever let a man stop your heart from loving, Bean," she tells me, as she flips the windblown skirts back down from her face. Everywhere Lou goes, she takes a photo with her wedding dress on. Mom scoffs and says it's just to prove she can still fit in it, but Lou told me the real story on the drive up.

"I had planned a future with him — one where we travelled and explored. I pictured sitting in our living room and showing friends slideshows of us at a ruined temple in Cambodia, or sitting astride an upturned dory on a Newfoundland beach. Home and away photos, you know?

"He took a lot from me, Bean, but I never will let him take my pictures away. And if I'm going to have to take them myself, I want what's missing to be bloody clear."

She always touched her right cheekbone when she spoke of him. That was where he hit her the worst. Even now, you can see how it's kinda misshapen, with an extra bump where it healed. Maybe it was broken.

She never went to the hospital. I sat on the stairs listening to her and Norma argue about it. Norma said she had to go, there could be internal injuries. She had to call the police. What if he did it to some other innocent girl?

Lou's voice got cold when she replied, "I said those same words to you. And where'd you go? Not the hospital. Not the police. You ran off to rid yourself of it and joined the convent. Hidden from the world. Like it was your shame to carry, not his."

I heard Norma sob and I wondered what they could be talking about.

I think I've figured it out now. That a man did own Aunt Norma. Back then I was a kid and I didn't get what they were saying. Watching Lou prancing around on the old battlements in her old wedding dress just now, it finally clicked.

Lou's on top of the cannon now and begging me to take another photo, her legs astride it and her white skirts swishing down its sides. Of course I take another photo. No one ever says no to Lou.

I wonder if Norma said no to that man. If she fought. Or did she just lie there and cry.

On the ride home I'll ask her about Norma. Ask her if what I suspect is true. Lou gets to wear white even though she's been wild and crazy and Norma, who never hurt anyone a day in her life, has to wear black — stained with someone else's sin.

I bet Lou even knows who he was.

I think my mother is jealous of her different and strong sisters. But I bet that every day Norma thinks of how she'd love to be rattling dishes while her kids listen and making perfect mounds of chip dip for the boring neighbours.

•••

DARA SQUIRES is a social media specialist with Best Boy Entertainment. An award-winning writer and parenting columnist, she writes in the midst of wrangling three kids and pouring more coffee. She has bright red hair.

The Nightingale

By Paul Whittle

Cuffer Prize 2012 Honourable Mention

On the way to the airport the radio plays "So this is Christmas, and what have you done?"

What have I not done? I have not: gotten Skype working on the blasted computer; gone to see her; looked into the logistics of spending the summer over there as planned.

See, I'd already been to London, I'd already been to see the Queen.

Let me take you by the hand
And lead you through the streets of London
I can show you something to change your mind

That was the song the Old Man used to sing. Sad songs to make you cry, and I could cry too. Nostalgia was like a genetic hereditary disease that I'd inherited from him and his lot.

When I'd come back from a year in London and another in Toronto, the Old Man had said: "you're changed."

And he was right.

No longer a pasty-faced bayman from Kilbride, I'd gone away like so many of my family and friends, come home like Odysseus, reunited with her, but then she left.

Penny's sending a text as she comes down the escalator at the airport.

"Hello honey," I say.

She kisses me on the cheek and looks around to see who's looking. She wears rubber boots, the kind of rubber boots that had once been only used by fishermen, now suddenly back in vogue in England since Kate Moss had worn them to Glastonbury and since farming organic root vegetables — a practice once relegated to the poor — is now all the rage.

Families erupt in explosions of joy throughout the arrivals area, fake Christmas wreaths hang over them and youngsters run around screeching like little Whos in Whoville. The bags are slow to come off the carousel.

"You think the new airport would have speeded this up. ... Can we stop at Mom's?" she says.

"Sure I guess, don't you want to drop off your bags, and we're going over later for supper, right?"

Penelope looks down at her phone again.

"How's the thesis?"

"I'm reading Dickens, 'Bleak House' and 'A Tale of Two Cities,' looking for the references about charity. I saved 'A Christmas Carol,' to get me in the spirit while I am here. It's all such a lot of work."

Finally the bags arrive and she sighs, most of the other folks don't seem to mind or notice any delay, they're still talking and yammering on in great anticipation of their own God-bless-us-everyone Christmas.

"Good ol' rain, drizzle and fog. I'm sure you didn't miss this." I say.

"You should have seen Oxford Street! I did some shopping there!"

She texts as we drive through the sodden streets, down over Portugal Cove Road, and then up the hill towards the old city, occasionally she looks up and makes a comment about plans for Christmas, but I'm disappointed that she is not more excited to be home. I had expected her joy to erupt like a blooming red poinsettia.

"Maurice just texted me a question about Keats."

She had not mentioned any Maurice before.

"Oh yeah, you're both working on Keats too?"

"Well tangentially. He's from Bristol," she said.

"What does that even mean?"

"He's at the British Museum right now."

Penny goes ahead of me into the house as I struggle to lift her bags as the Eastern Star hangs over the towers of the Basilica.

"Full of presents, no doubt," I say, with the familiar teasing voice that we often used with each other, and all throughout this place, a tone to remind her where she is, to remind her that she is home.

"Mostly books," she says, "it's a chance to read."

"Christmas time is here," the old Charlie Brown standard plays on the radio as we sit down on the chesterfield and drink a bottle of wine, chat about her thesis and the difference in the weather between here and there. Mostly, we drink, nervously feeling how it is to be in each other's space again.

She lays her head on my chest, closes her eyes. When she wakes I take her by the hand and we go upstairs, climb on top of the bed, clothed, negotiate where to look at each other and how to move, gauge what was then and what is now, as if time could be recovered with enough belief in the present.

"I missed you so much" I say, into her ear, close and dear, trying to bridge the distance between us.

Penny turns away and goes to the bathroom. I creep over the hardwood and I hear her whimpering inside, low and pitiable, like a bird, and I remembered a scene from "The Odyssey": Tereus cuts out Philomena's tongue, so she turns herself into a nightingale and flies away.

I knew the best thing to do was to get back into bed and pretend that things had not changed.

We had to get through Christmas.

•••

PAUL WHITTLE *was born and raised in St. John's. He began writing while completing a degree in English literature in 1999. Since then he has won Newfoundland and Labrador Arts and Letters' awards for poetry and prose. His writing has been published in Tickleace, The Newfoundland Quarterly, and in "The Backyards of Heaven." In 2012 he had a residency at the Banff Arts Centre to work on a collection of short stories. One story in the collection, "Everything is What it is," was shortlisted for the 2009 CBC literary awards. He holds a master's degree in English literature at Memorial University, where he works in marketing and communications.*

Before There Was Air

By Robert Chafe

You have been walking at night. I sometimes hear you, jiggling through the rack of keys two rooms away, the warmth of you still in the bed. Some nights I get up and make it to the window in time to see you turn the corner at the end of the street, the amber of the overhead and that tight white winter coat. In the porch, your mukluk-style boots gone, a puddle of dirty salt water in their wake.

I turn the heat up a bit to compensate, and eventually go back to sleep. I worry that you won't come back, that the city, its size and darkness, will somehow finally claim you. I think of calling the cops. But you are always there in the morning when I wake up. You sleep longer then, longer than normal. I make strong coffee, sometimes even a hot breakfast, try to tease an ounce of personal warmth from you. Some mornings, sitting across the table from me, your breakfast untouched, you can't be summoned back from the place you have gone. No matter what I do. So far away, and going further each night.

It wasn't always this way.

Before we were here, we were there. A tiny town all but in the ocean itself, a fishplant, a grocery store. A gas station in the summer months. You and me we had worked at that grocery store, that gas station. You and me, we had wanted more. We saw better for ourselves in that silent kind of way, in a way that wouldn't hurt our parents' feelings. And when we got to be an age where what we were doing and planned to do was a constant matter of speculation in that grocery line, we started talking about places that we saw on TV, cities with teams, jerseys we wore. "I don't want anyone in our business," I said. We were being suffocated. And you and me, we like to breathe.

That was in the spring of the year, and that winter previous it had snowed like the end of days. And nights when it was too rough and cold to make the 10-minute walk home, I had taken to staying with you in the unfinished basement apartment of your parents' house. That wallpaper mural, the desert island with the palm trees, it was fooling no one.

The day your father went walking, it was a fine one for a change. He started out after lunch, a few good hours of sun left and his rabbit snares unchecked for days. He put on his Ski-Doo boots, his heaviest coat and walked through the part in the trees at the back of the yard. Darkness came home but your father didn't. Your mother told us she wasn't worried, but she stood at the kitchen sink washing the same pot for a half-hour, avoiding her reflection in the window. Around 10 o'clock that night you asked me to go get Tom Kelland down the way and I did and your mother got angry at me and Tom when we got back. Tom, his orange hunting jacket, his big sealskin mitts, they seemed to cement for her that your dad was in trouble. Within the half hour Tom and the b'ys were gone, out through the same part in the woods, their heavy flashlights crashing through the bottoms of the snow-covered trees.

Your mother settled into fret then, a slow pace through the house, hand capped sideways over her mouth. You suggested a game of cards to get her off her feet. "A way to pass the time," you said, and even I thought it in poor taste. Your mother gave you a look, angry and hurt, her fear bubbling out in predictable ways, and you started to cry. And there I was then, my woman in the bathroom, sink running to cover her sobs, and her mother in the kitchen, face buried in her hands and shaking with the release of it all.

And so it went, until nearly two o'clock in the morning when a lick of light on the ceiling told us something was happening out the back window. All of us to it then and we saw Gerald Hartery coming through the long yard with your father on his back. Tom Kelland and five or six others coming along behind, a laugh on the air, a joke or punch line landed and the men telling us in their walk and manner that everything was all right. You father slung like a knapsack, hanging on, his arms clasped around Gerald's neck, and his feet dragging in the knee-deep snow. Gerald wore himself out 10 yards from the house and your father was passed over to Gus Kenny for the final stretch. Your mother ran to the back door, leaping relief altogether and let fly with a string of curses, the steam coming out of the open house behind her.

Your father was propped next to the wood stove, a blanket on his lap and his blue feet soaked in a warm tub of water. He told us then about the snow squall setting in, and the loss of his tracks, and that big pine that he always used to mark the dense path back to the house and how it must have ended up in someone's living room for the holidays because he couldn't spot it after four hours of trying. His feet had gotten the best of him, feeling wet and cold and sore, and then nothing at all, and it got to be that he himself was afraid of where it would all end up. He sat at the bottom of a tree, sang himself a song, loud enough that he could muster the faint hope that it might be heard. It eventually was.

For all your mother's anger at the beginning and the end of it, when Tom Kelland tried to leave the house that night empty-handed she didn't make it easy. A good loaf of bread, the bottle of your father's good whisky we had brought him in from our last trip to town. She hugged him then, Tom Kelland. Your father there staring at the fire through the stove's glass door.

That was the place we left. That was the place we couldn't take anymore, that suffocated us.

I was the one that told you I wanted to move away from it. I said I hated it there and you said there's a grand seduction in defining yourself in opposition to the one thing you know. All the same I kept throwing around words like opportunity and future, fat empty words that were difficult to counter. You loved me enough not to try. You loved me back then, when we came here, and before. And so now, with your tired eyes in the morning and the question of where you have been, who you have been with, always on my lips, I just try to silence myself and remember that. You loved me once. Once I was worth following. Once I was worth walking towards.

...

ROBERT CHAFE is a St. John's-based writer whose work as a playwright has been seen across Canada, the U.K., Australia and in the States. He was shortlisted for the Governor General's Award for Drama ("Tempting Providence" and "Butler's Marsh") in 2004, and won the award for "Afterimage" in 2010.

Coming Home

By Amanda Stephen

It's a midnight cattle run on Air Canada from Halifax to Deer Lake. The plane is smooth over black water, under a clear summer sky, but I'm sitting in 3A with a spear in my gut. It's a cold, hard-knotted wrenching: a pain that causes me to sweat down my spine and in other uncomfortable places. It's the ache of adult me, coming home.

I'm not a nervous flyer. But somewhere between growing up, moving away and returning home I got the sickness. It's a kind of white-knuckled junk sickness, like coming off some vile beast that I've been riding hard towards abuse; always with bile in my throat and my bowels threatening to let go. Sometime after leaving for education and life elsewhere, the journey home became less a relief and more a coming down. It happens without fail now: my travels are clear until I hit the Halifax hub. That's when the mouth-biting starts, the twitching of nervous fingers, the heart racing too fast for me to keep up. They page my name — last call before Newfoundland, last chance to turn around.

I excuse myself and squeeze my way toward the lone washroom. The tightness of the closet is comforting; it gives me space to hold on, to try and maintain. I have a snort of the over-the-counter cocktail I prepared this morning: caffeine, ibuprofen, T3. It's less about the pills hitting my bloodstream and more about the burning I feel when I fill my nasal passages; the raw grit is comforting. It's bread for the journey.

The urge to fly back into the cabin, wrench open the emergency exit and fling myself into the night is overwhelming. But I resist and content myself with solitary confinement — just me and my reflection. Watery eyes, running nose, a lump in the throat. I flush my mouth with water over and over and over, trying to rid it of the stale dryness that comes with the longing and fear of the sickness. It's the feeling I used to get when I was afraid I wasn't going to be able to score. That panic when an exchange is about to fall through: when a dealer doesn't show or the money doesn't come. Junk worry creeping into my bones. But for now, I've contained it. I've maintained. I head back to my seat.

There's something terrible and familiar about returning to the place where you first cultivated your habits. I'm headed back to the town where I had my first binge. Where a 12-year-old version of me sat in someone's toilet-less basement and drank Tia Maria from a water bottle. Where I sucked back on my first grass, and latched on to an ugly boy with beautiful prescriptions. The restaurant where I bought my first gram of cocaine is an eight-minute walk from my house. The basement where I gnawed into a wall and fell into frenzies of ecstasy is three minutes more. Familiar corners, trees and benches: all with a drug history of their own. Stepping stones, mile-markers, signposts on a gravel highway.

The man in the Blue Jays cap in 3C bought me a beer in my absence. I think he understands I need it, though not the extent of my want. I throw my head back and chug. There's half a probability I'll be forced to vomit it into the neatly folded paper bag in front of me. But I take my chances; I have no other choice. Anything that might suppress the sickness must be consumed.

I know baseball cap is fresh from Fort Mac. Half of the plane is: mostly men coming home after a term in the camps. Come back to build castles in villages, to throw money around for a stint until they're called back again. My sources tell me their new lifestyles have caused growth in the drug scene back home. Alberta trucks have come home with Alberta money and Alberta cocaine. They've even brought back enough Special K to keep things interesting — just enough to keep the demons in the bay. City money means city needs, and the small towns dotting my coastline are struggling to deliver. I used to think that the fastest-moving product in the west was worms in St. Jude's; now it's a Technicolor of matchbox-sized baggies.

The sickness is about knowing what's waiting when I touch down. It's not just the drugs; the people are habit-forming too. It's about falling back into old crowds, old routines, old vices, without hesitation. Jagged rocks support small communities all along the coastline, communities like my own, where no face is a stranger. When everyone knows who you are, there's no escaping your former self. There are no masks in outports, and maybe that's what I love and hate about it all. I abhor the church, but pray every night for the same reason — the routine cradles my soul. Consistency keeps the shakes away.

I shudder into my seat and wish I was coming home with honourable intentions. I wish it was enough to just love the island in its purest unadulterated form. Hair heavy and gritty with the salt-soaked air should be enough. Fingers stained and sticky with blue, picking through the bramble. Welts from mosquito kisses on my neck, chest, legs. Rough rock beneath my feet and nothing holding me back: it used to be enough. But at some point I developed a few more itches, a few more scrapes, a few more bruises. And suddenly, the island just didn't satisfy.

My stomach drops and I retch as the plane hits the tarmac. We jolt, screech, coast into the lights of Deer Lake. In one swift movement I reopen the wound, turning on my phone prematurely and furiously reaching out to my local network. Just like that, four months of relative sobriety have fallen overboard. In the next 24 hours I'll be at a bar 15 minutes from the airport to pick up the special of the week; it's all over, and I know it.

The wind catches me, holds me teetering at the top of the stairs for a moment, before I start downward. Bag and hat clutched in hand, I head toward the orange lights of the terminal. It's a death march — heavy and sinking. This one ends, not in the grave, but in the arms of my father. He's there waiting, always, just inside the doors. He's skinnier, maybe frail, but I can't help throw myself, wrecked with grief, into his arms. I heave and shake and crumple, squeezing my eyes shut. Clinging to the stiff fabric of his jacket, it soaks with liquid from my mouth, nose and forehead. He smells clean and whole and old, and I feel childlike. I feel unworthy of his embrace, and of the land we're standing on.

He knows. By God, does he know. His smoothing palm warms my back, lets me know that it's broken, but that it's OK. He can fix it. We can fix it.

"I know," he soothes. "I know. There's nothing like coming home."

•••

AMANDA STEPHEN, *21, grew up in Pasadena and is fresh off four years in Ottawa completing her bachelor of journalism degree. Today she makes her home on Fogo Island, where she is replanting her family roots.*

✓Home

By Elizabeth Wright

I am on my way to my brother's house in Long Point. It's been 10 years, but I remember every bend in this road. I'm here because last month I saw a photograph on someone's desk at work.

It was beautifully composed; a bride and groom in a flower-filled garden, the deep red clapboard of the house behind them, set against the serene blue backdrop of the Atlantic. And off to the right, an old woman sitting on a kitchen chair, smiling at the couple.

I managed to ask my colleague where the picture was taken.

"We had a destination wedding," she said, pausing as she picked up the photograph, carefully wiping the glass with her sleeve. "You know, everyone travels to the wedding, and then you, like, stay on after. So you're getting a trip. And we went to Newfoundland!

"It was so awesome! The people were so friendly, and funny! We even went to a kitchen party, and met amazing people, like this old lady. She was, like, the midwife there and, what's her name now, wait, Aunt something. … I think she's, like, related to the photographer?"

She didn't have to tell me the old lady's name. Her name is Jane Lewis. She's 87 years old and she spent her entire working life behind the Woolworth's bakery counter in Corner Brook. She is my aunt, and she lives in a long-term care facility in Clarenville.

That's when I decided to visit my brother. And that's why I'm on my way to Long Point now, instead of spending my leave repainting my condo.

I arrive mid-afternoon. The house looks tidy. Birch junks are stacked on the bridge, alongside a white enamelled bucket and a pair of rubber boots. There's even a black and white cat, gazing impassively at me as I come up the path and walk around to the back porch. The back of the house is a different colour — burnt orange. Wade is here, unplugging what looks like a giant fan next to a clothesline full of quilts.

He doesn't see me until I say his name.

"Susan," he says. He knew I was coming, but I don't think he wants to see me.

He takes me inside. It is nothing like Nan's house.

One summer, Dad and my uncles renovated this house. They cased the whole thing in white vinyl siding, replaced all the windows and put in fake wood panelling and carpets.

That's all gone. The downstairs is transformed, with a stamped tin ceiling, sanded wood floors and painted walls. All of the light fixtures are moulded glass. The house looks to have been restored to museum standards: "Outport Home. Circa 1923." There's no sign of anything remotely modern.

We sit at a table in the kitchen, talking about lots of nothing.

I can't wait any longer. "Where did you get this stuff?" I say.

"What?" He shifts a bit in his chair.

"Where did all this come from? Daybeds and woodstoves and washbasins."

"Well, I went to estate sales, and I made some of it. Woodworker up near Glovertown made the daybed."

"Where's Nan's stuff?"

"At the dump, mostly — it was junk." He gives me a puzzled look.

"Did you want that stuff?" he continues, defiant now. "A spoon rack in the shape of Newfoundland?"

"Oh very funny, Wade. That's not what I meant and you know it."

"No, I don't. Why did you decide to visit me? Why have you been quietly freaking out since you got here?"

"Let's start with this house. It looks like a National Historic Site. And what's up with the outside? The front's red and the back's orange!"

He sighs. "It gives customers a choice of background for photos. And before you ask, that's a wind machine out back. I use it for shots with the quilts — I can't always count on the wind blowing the right way. People like that in the background sometimes; it's like the ads."

"Right. Got any redheaded kids to run around in the foreground?"

"No, Susan. No kids." It takes me a minute to realize that I've gone too far, but he lets it go.

He sighs again. "It's usually tourists, mostly weddings — it pays the bills — people want the local stuff. And I do the B&B thing, and boat tours with Neil."

"What about Aunt Jane? How could you use her like that?"

"Sometimes I bring her down with me for the weekend. It takes her back to when she was living here with great-grandmother ... and, yes, I have put her in some of the pictures."

"No kidding. There's a woman in Ottawa who thinks she had the oldest living midwife in Newfoundland in her wedding picture."

It gets really, really quiet then, until Wade shrugs and says, "What odds, Susan, anyway?"

"What odds? What are you, a professional Newfoundlander?"

"I'm a Newfoundlander."

"You're a professional Newfoundlander. You sing for your supper. I bet you have a little piece on the loss of your country. Do you have a moratorium story? Oh wait, no you don't, because computer programmers living in Ontario weren't actually affected by the moratorium, were they?"

"Right — and you've never let people know that you're from Newfoundland, used that to get you noticed."

"No, as a matter of fact, I haven't."

But of course I have, when it's been useful. I don't do it anymore. The market's been saturated, in my opinion.

"So why did you come racing up here to tell me off?"

"Because this is ... manufactured authenticity. You never liked Long Point. The one time you went fishing off the wharf, Dad had to come get you because you were scared of the sculpin you caught!"

Wade's hand slams down on the table.

"Oh shut up, Susan! That was 40 years ago! This house gives me peace. I lost everything, and this place pulled me back.

"There is beauty and grace here Susan, and someone has to keep safe what we had. We did once have what you see here. Maybe it wasn't just like this — I mean of course it wasn't, but what's wrong with the way I live?

"So if I need to sing for my supper — so be it. I'll give 'em what they want — photographs and kitchen parties and boat tours and whatever else the Department of Tourism dreams up. Because by September they're all gone. And I've got eight months of the year to myself."

That's the most Wade's ever said to me about anything. He's right. He's decided to be a Newfoundlander and I've decided not to.

It's a long time before either of us speaks.

"Want some tea, Wade?"

"Sure."

I resist the urge to ask if there's a tea doll somewhere that I need to open.

"Tea's in the cupboard," he says. "There's a kettle there too — I don't have the stove going on when I'm by myself."

And there in the cupboard is Nan's tea canister — chipped white ceramic, decorated with a goose wearing a frilly bonnet, a pink ribbon round its neck.

"You might as well keep that out on the counter," Wade says. "Easier to reach."

∙∙∙

ELIZABETH WRIGHT has lived in St. John's with her family for the past 11 years. She is an epidemiologist with the Public Health Agency of Canada.

I Don't Dream of Genie

By Chad Pelley

What these kids don't know, as I bounce them on my knee, is that I'm a woman in a Santa suit. Not only is Santa not real, but my name is Sherry, I'm Jewish, and I wear a 32B instead of boxer briefs. But pull a beard over my delicate cheekbones and you'd swear I was just another downtrodden man, temping part-time for the Avalon Mall. I've always felt I had the sunken eyes of a defeated male, and pulling off a Santa impersonation proves it.

It also proves that you can know nothing, when looking a stranger in the eye. I don't know what these kids want until they're knifing their behinds into my gym-taut thighs and shouting it into my ear. They think the louder they yell it, the better their chances are of getting it. So, at night, my left ear rings into my pillow, chanting me to sleep. But the scratchy fake beard is the worst; it leaves a rash, some acne. Another reason I'm all alone at 33.

What I like about being secretly Santa, is I like hearing other people are longing for something too; even if it's just new toys. The sign in the Avalon Mall food court said, "Mall Santa wanted," and I saw it as a clipped sentence: I wondered what it was Santa wanted … and didn't get.

When I applied, I stepped into the room, and they looked over my shoulder to the empty doorway like I was only there to accompany a husband or a son who never did walk through the door. I sat down with a look on my face that said, scream sexism these days and they'll give you more than a Santa suit. Not that I played that card. I just needed a simple, second, temporary job.

It would sound more human and strife-y to say I took this Santa gig to help fund my cat's leukemia treatment, but the truth is I took it to reimburse myself for a trip to Tennessee, to attend a three-day lucid dreaming seminar. The trip put four grand on my MasterCard, and has my mother worried about me. And I never learned a God damned thing at that session.

What happened was I couldn't sleep one night, and there was this made-for-TV movie on. In the movie, an adorable geezer — with eyebrows bushier than squirrel tails — went to a spiritual witchy woman to summon his dead wife. How dumb is that, right? But I dreamt of Gene that night, my ex. I dreamt everything was all right. I dreamt we were at his mother's place in Rocky Harbour and the sun was a lantern; the whole six o'clock sky was a pumpkin, freckled by the black sickles of tern wings. He was cooking me scrambled eggs with fresh herbs, and I could smell it, sharp as glass in my nose. I had two hands wrapped around a mug of coffee, to take the morning chill out of my hands. It's something I always did, so he'd made the water extra hot before pouring it into the French press. But then I woke up. Before we could share one more moment, where I felt so totally his.

I woke up and there was an infomercial on, blaring about lucid dreaming techniques: Channel your dream life through lucid dreaming ... with Dr. Lee Markus's bestselling book. But who has the patience to read a 400-page book? I Googled "lucid dreaming" and bought a package I saw in the Google Ads bar. The thought of being able to direct your own dreams at night, and decide on the cast, the plot, the setting; slow motion, instant replays. No-holds-barred sex scenes. I wanted to crawl under my sheets at night and slip into a fantasy life. I wanted to dream of Gene again.

But even the flight was long and tumultuous. Two stopovers, and the kind of turbulence that made me wish I'd watched the flight safety video. The only thing I retained from the first day's lecture was that many dreams turn lucid when the dreamer realizes some improbability, like you're flying in your dream. Once your sleep-self knows it's dreaming, you can take control of the dream.

So that night before bed, to trigger a flying dream, I watched all the flying-related movies I could think of. Like "Top Gun" and the first two "Superman" movies. But no luck. No improbable dream sequences. No dreams of Genie. I couldn't even remember what I dreamt about when I woke up the next morning. But that Christopher Reeve: what was a handsome man in his day.

Another way to tell your sleep-self that it's dreaming is to almost wake up, mid-dream, and then fall back into the dream immediately. But try rigging a big bowl to tip over in your kitchen at three in the morning — to half wake you — without being some kind of engineer. There was supposed to be a science to lucid dreaming. Steps to follow, like how adding soda powder to vinegar will, and always will, result in fizzy success. I didn't even stay for the last seminar on Sunday night, about "The MILD Technique." I went to a cheap Lebanese restaurant and got food poisoning.

I spent my flight home throwing up from both ends in a cramped Air Canada washroom, with half the plane listening in disgust. Then I hung out in the bathroom until we landed. I didn't want the person in 44B feeling gross or bad for me.

My sister picked me up at the airport. She didn't even say hello. She said, "It's time to move on." I asked her if she had any gum in her purse, and she said, "Gene is long gone."

When people say "just move on," it sounds the way a shrugged shoulder looks: ambivalent, and lacking in compassion. The mind is a boat, anchored in desire, and the only thing that can cut that rope is time. I'm no more ready to move on than I am Santa Claus. It was only last Christmas when Gene told me there was another girl. Someone from his gym. I remember running away from the words. Heading for the front door. In a nightgown. When he tried to restrain me, we went whirlpooling down a spiraling staircase together, like fish caught in a drain.

His last words as he stood in our porch, bleeding, bruised, and clutching a snapped wrist, were cruel and exact. He'd taken aim with them, and shot me down. Punctuated them with a slammed door.

I told no one about my broken toe. Not even a doctor. And I think of Gene every time that badly healed bone hums with pain in bed at night. I think of him every time one of these hope-filled kids steps on my Santa boot, on their way back to their mother, and the simple life they think is waiting for them.

• • •

CHAD PELLEY'S fiction has been recognized by 10 awards. He is the author of "Away from Everywhere" (2009), which is being adapted for film, and "Every Little Thing" (2013). He also runs the literary blog Salty Ink.

Just Wait Till I Tells You

By Michael Finn

Oh my dear, just wait till I tells you, you won't believe me. … No, you won't. … Just wait, I'll get to it by and by…

Anyway, "Never again," I told Victor, "never again." I said to Victor on the way home, I said, "Victor, next year they all gets a bit o' money or a gift card from Wal-Mart, or I'll send 'em all socks and toques, knit 'em all meself if I has to, but I can guarantee you one thing, Victor, I can guar-an-tee you one thing, this is the last, and I means it too" — oh I was right riled up, my dear, right riled I was — "this is the ab-so-lute godforsaken last time I does any Christmas shoppin' in town. The last time. Never again."

Oh, my dear, you won't believe it. … And you knows me and Victor now, maid, don't you? Here we is now, both in our 70s — our 70s, now mind you — just lookin' for a place to park at the mall, like you would, hey? And you knows what 'tis like now my dear, don't you? … Yes, o' course you do, my dear, 'tis madness, madness! 'Deed it is my dear. … Yes, we prob'ly should've stayed home out of it, been better off. Poor Victor, my dear, his blood pressure is gone right up, had to pour 'nself three fingers o' whisky right when we got through the door, he was that upset 'bout it. … Oh, he's calmed down a bit now, girl, thank God.

Anyway, there we was, like I was sayin', just lookin' for a parkin' spot at the mall, and we was drivin' around and drivin' around for 15, 20 minutes … oh my dear, don't be talkin'.… Maggoty? My dear, bumper-to-bumper the whole time. Matter of fact, Victor was that poisoned with it all I was tempted to tell 'n to forget about it, 'cause I could see the veins poppin' out on the sides of his head, and I was afraid he'd take a stroke right there in the Avalon Mall parkin' lot, and it'd be the end of 'n. But then we was just after makin' maybe a dozen turns around the lot, when a fella in a spot just a few feet ahead starts backin' out. So

Victor puts on his signal, like you're s'posed to. An' buddy in the car backin' out waves to 'n, like he was sayin', "Come on my son, she's all yours." An' Victor waves back, an' I waves too, an' the other fella nods an' smiles, right friendly-like.

So we was feelin' pretty good, then, 'cause I figured we had a good spot, maid, 'cause 'twas not too far from the mall entrance, so's we wouldn't have to carry our parcels too far, hey? Anyway, buddy backs out an' he goes on, an' just ahead of us we sees this other buddy in this great big rig, one o' them old Hummers, but he's not signallin' or nothin', so Victor is just turnin' to park in the empty spot when this Hummer fella turns right fast an' sharp an' cuts Victor off. So Victor brakes right sudden so's not to hit buddy, an' both of us looks up at him in the cab of his rig, grinnin' down right saucy at us. An' I could see the blood start boilin' in Victor's veins, an' he looks up right hard at buddy — you knows Victor, don't you, when he gets all upset? — an' before Victor can say anything, this, this arsehole. ... yes my dear, that's the only word to describe him, this arsehole hoists up his middle finger an'... well, you knows what he says, hey maid? Even though we couldn't hear him, 'twas pretty clear what he was sayin'.

So Victor shoved down his door handle, my dear, an' he was just about to get out when I says to him, "Victor, now you stay put. I'll handle this," 'cause to tell the truth, girl, I was afraid Victor'd haul off an' belt him, an' then we'd be in a fine mess, 'cause as mad as I was 'bout it all I knew that buddy hadn't done nothin' illegal, he was just bein' rude an' ignorant, an' 'tis no crime to be rude an' ignorant to people, now, is it maid?

So I gets out an' I goes over to his rig, an' I sees him lookin' ahead, pretendin' I wasn't there. I reaches up an' taps his window, an' he rolls her down an' looks at me. So I says to him —an' maid, I was as polite as could be — I says, "Excuse me sir, did you not see my husband signal to indicate his intention to turn into this space?"

The next thing I knows, he's openin' his door — almost knocked me over, he did — and climbin' out without so much as a word or a glance at me, an' he starts to walk towards the mall. "Excuse me, Sir, but I asked you a question just now, if you don't mind," I says, a bit louder this time.

An' girl, that's when he stops an' turns to me an' says — an' maid, I never had anyone ever before in all my days say anything as rude and filthy as what he said — he says, "Merry fuckin' Christmas, bitch." … I swear to God, girl! His exact words! Can you imagine? Can you imagine? "Merry fuckin' Christmas, bitch!" An then he just turns an' walks on …

Oh he was all dressed up, my dear, shirt 'n' tie, nice coat, dress pants, clean-shaven fella, hair all combed an' neat. … Yes my dear, just turned an' walked away. Could o' been goin' to church for all anyone knew. … Oh no, maid, I didn't tell Victor what he said, 'cause Victor would have gone after him. You knows Victor. Don't you tell him either, girl, for God's sake. … Anyway, when I got back in the car I just told Victor it was no use, an' I won't repeat what he said — you knows Victor, so you can just imagine — so we went out to the Village after he calmed down, even though 'twasn't where we really wanted to go.

But I was thinkin' about it on the way home, girl, I was thinkin' that St. John's is not like it used to be, an' they can keep their oil an' their Costco an' their new housing developments an' all the rest of it, 'cause if this is what it means, well, what in the name o' God is the use of it? And like I said to Victor, next year I think I'll knit some socks an' so on, send the grandchildren a bit o' money, maybe …

Yes, maid, you're right, a good cup o' tea is what I needs, an' maybe I'll put a drop o' Victor's whisky into it too. … The same to you, my dear … yes, we'll be seein' you at midnight mass. … An' a Merry Christmas to you too, maid, a Merry Christmas to you too.

***

MICHAEL FINN was born and raised in Grand Falls. He now lives in St. Bernard's-Jacques Fontaine on the Burin Peninsula. He makes the occasional foray into town.

Leaving

By Deborah Whelan

"Buyer must love roses?" The real estate agent blinked rapidly and fiddled with her pen. "That's … unusual. You're limiting your market share. Not everyone wants the responsibility of a garden. People don't have time."

"I'll make the price competitive," I said. "It's a beautiful space. It deserves someone who'll care for it."

It worked. This morning, the agent's voice is a series of exclamation points. "They've accepted your counteroffer! Your house is sold! Congratulations!"

It's done. I can leave and all the pain will stay here, with the house. I hang up the phone. I think of the Ativan in my bedside table; the crutch is beckoning. But this morning I am Buddha. I breathe and smile and email the family the news and sit and stare at the screen. My laptop hums. I could make tea, perhaps eat toast. I don't think I ate yesterday. Is it too early for Grand Marnier and coffee? Blood swooshes in zigzag patterns behind my eyes.

The stairs creak and groan behind me. I glance around, expecting to see Kenny, his sleep-creased face, his smile shiny with braces. No one there. The air ripples as if it aches to create him, just there on the third step.

The old gentleman who sold me this house said he believed the stairs had arthritis like him. He had a lot to say before he could let go. "You'll have to replace the storm windows," he said, "and watch the door locks. You might need to get those little cans of spray to clear them in the winter — they tend to freeze up." He pushed back the curtains and pointed toward the expanse of garden. "And there's some real pretty tulips in the spring.

Since my wife's gone, I don't do much with it but there's all kinds of stuff out there, all coming up at different times so there's always something nice to look at. Margaret planned it that way. That's her name. Margaret. She planted a rose called the Princess Margaret and then one for me called Eric the Red. That's me, Eric." He chuckled and wiped at his eyes. "Then when the children came along, there was a special rose for each of them. She went and named our children after roses. God love Margaret."

The papers are signed. The house belongs to someone else now. My oldest sister emails, shouting "CONGRATULATIONS BUT IT MUST BE SAD TOO, IN A WAY. LOTS OF MEMORIES, EH?" Why does she need to say "sad" and "memories"? She always has to bring emotion into every damn thing; why couldn't she just say "GREAT"?

Julia emails. "Wow, Mom, that was superfast! When do you have to be out of there? I'd kinda like to come home for a weekend so I can sleep in my old room once more." Sad emoticon.

Julia has a new room in a white-walled apartment in downtown Calgary, complete with handsome engineer and engagement ring. Her room here will be filled by a stranger who will push her spirit out the window, echoes of goodnights and sleeptights swept clean from the corners.

I answer. "Jules, my darling, the closing is the end of the month and there's no bed in your room anymore; that all disappeared on Kijiji, the white bureau with the pink flowery handles, too. What I haven't sold is staying with the house."

The house that Margaret surrounded with roses: the yard had almost enough room for the children, although separate planets would have worked better. Kenny was only 12 then, and I was amazed at how naturally he took over where Margaret had left off, loving and nursing the veritable rose forest that climbed out of the loamy soil. Julia preferred soccer and used the space between Margaret and Eric as her goal. Kenny dug and pruned and weeded, and Julia destroyed with each errant kick.

Julia's email chimes in. "What about Kenny's stuff? Is it still there? Have you sold him, too?"

I know she means "sold that." And I can smell her pain, even in lower case. I still need to clean out his room. My condo in the Middle Battery is new and shiny like the plastic lemons in the stainless steel fruit bowl on its white counter. It has no room for his stuff. The condo comes furnished. Memory-free.

But I do not know how to start. I could begin by taking the books down, all his much-loved volumes of poetry and mystery perfectly aligned on white shelves that he and I built into the walls above his desk. But I can only walk in and lie on his bed and hold his pillow tight against my face. Grief runs its fingers up and down my spine, paralyzing me. After eight months and 13 days, Kenny's room still smells like him, like warm sun on bed sheets. That's all I have left.

"I'm going to call the Salvation Army to come and pick up his things," I write back. She'll know I'm lying, that I cannot stuff boxes with his tennis racquet, his "I Refuse to Star in your Psychodrama" T-shirt, his teddy bear that he pretended he didn't sleep with, and let someone else touch them, wear them.

The roses are doing well. I thought by now they'd be wilting, or have fungus or mildew or blight, all the things Kenny seemed to know about without having to learn them. But they've budded out and some of the early ones are in full bloom. When I dare to look out in the garden I sometimes see him digging behind the honeysuckle arbour — just for a heartbeat, then the air swallows him up.

He was so happy in the garden. I thought he was happy all the time. He fooled me. What kind of mother doesn't know her child wants to die? In October, we sat on the cold stone steps in the backyard and he talked about how to care for the roses, like I was the child and he was the parent. He went on and on about mulching and wrapping the hybrids for the winter, and pruning and feeding in the spring, and I listened and glowed at his passion, never knowing he was passing the torch to me, the one who knew nothing about gardens except that he kept ours beautiful. But I don't deserve to touch it.

What kind of mother doesn't see the pain her child suffers? He smiled for me, didn't tell about the gay boy taunts and the disgusting Photoshopped pictures. Even when I found him, all I could do was scream and pull at the knots in the rope and try to get him down. I tried to breathe for him and beat at his chest but the paramedic took my hands in hers and said, "It's too late, my dear, he's gone." I covered him with his baby quilt, with its appliquéd yellow satin ducks and blue and white sailboats, the one I'd saved for his first child. That's all I could do.

All I can do now is find someone to take care of his roses.

•••

DEBORAH WHELAN lives in Heart's Delight-Islington. She is a member of the Writers' Alliance of Newfoundland and Labrador, an avid short-story writer and has been shortlisted for the Cuffer Prize three times.

Loss of the Aeolus

By Ian Hutchings

Jim Cochrane steers the boat's wheel under a threatening sky.

He and the crew had been battling to stay afloat since the storm rumbled overhead 20 minutes ago, obscuring a beautiful sunny day.

The longliner Aeolus is out on a crab run. They are only supposed to be out for a night, and then return to port with their catch.

As the blue water darkens into a metallic grey and starts to lop, the crew continues their work with wary eyes on the horizon.

The situation deteriorates as each minute ticks by. The deck is flooding, being filled by the torrential rainfall. There is water spilling into the engine room. Cochrane has already ordered a mayday.

A gale blows up. A squall of wind swipes the water like a massive trident, the transfer of energy churning up enormous waves. The waves chop muscularly toward the boat. Cochrane had been in a few gales before, and even a hurricane or two, but nothing like this.

Cochrane is the boat's skipper. He quakes with dread inside, but tries to appear outwardly calm and commanding for the sake of his crew. He holds the wheel with a firm grip and issues orders to his men.

A sudden large swell from behind raises the stern and he sees through the front window a preview of the murky depths as a giant wave crashes into the bridge head-on. The boat rocks and swivels 200 degrees off-course. All these years of experience as a fisherman and skipper and there isn't much he can do.

"Oates, radio Halifax again!" Cochrane bellows over the raging surf and lashing rain.

Cochrane's first mate, Ted Oates, radios the Halifax Subsea Centre with a mayday for the second time, and curses the feds for shutting down the St. John's rescue centre. There is no sign of any other vessels on radar. The Aeolus would be under the waves long before anyone arrived.

A yell from the deck as the water soaks the men. Their feet abruptly slide down a 45-degree angle. The crab traps skitter off the deck into the water, freeing their prey. The engine floods and sputters dead. The lights and navigational computer blink out. They are adrift as the colossal waves toss them like a toy in a bathtub.

Making an executive decision, Cochrane tells Oates to get the men and himself off the boat. As skipper, Cochrane will stay aboard until the last possible minute. Perhaps the storm will clear. The digital weather station is offline, but the manual barometer is still indicating low pressure.

As the longliner lolls from port to starboard amid crests and troughs of large waves, Jim thinks wistfully of his wife Kat and son Jon back in Trout River. She has always been prepared for the danger of losing him to the sea, but is anyone truly prepared? She may have to face the possibility in the next few minutes. Jon will get the full story and understand as he grows up. Kat is a strong woman and can take care of herself, but Jim's greatest regret is that he won't be around for Jon. A tear rolls down his cheek, masked by the rain and mist.

A massive wave rolls the boat along its central axis, the stabilizers fail, and the crew goes into freefall. Cochrane loses his grip on the wheel and tumbles through the hatch with a lion-like roar of defiance.

Cochrane, Oates, and the men plunge into the Atlantic.

All Cochrane sees is an endless hazy grey, and feels an intense shock of cold. He was never a religious man, but as his consciousness fades, he begins to pray. He prays to God to take care of his crew and to help his wife and son have a good life. The grey blackens into oblivion.

•••

Oates bobs to the surface, and treads water as he looks around in horror. His longliner Aeolus is rolling on its side like the Costa Concordia and slowly disappearing. No sign of Cochrane and the others.

As the bridge sinks, he could hear the radio faintly crackling. " … Aeolus Aeolus Aeolus … this is Halifax-Halifax-Halifax. Received mayday …" then burbles as the Aeolus goes under.

Oates is alone on the suddenly calming Atlantic Ocean. It's eerily quiet. The clouds break up and the sun comes out. Deep blue water stretches to every horizon. The EPIRB releases from the plummeting bridge and floats up.

Feeling very small and insignificant, he clings to the blinking beacon, awaiting the assistance that may not arrive in time.

•••

IAN HUTCHINGS is from Carbonear and resides in Corner Brook. He graduated from College of the North Atlantic in 2004 with a diploma in journalism and spent five years working in the Northwest Territories and Alberta. In 2011, he returned to College of the North Atlantic to study environmental technology.

My Candy Girl

By Scott Bartlett

Wylie Ryan places the bottle of beets on the conveyor belt. It glides toward the cashier, stopping abruptly and nearly tipping over onto the barcode scanner.

"Is that all?" the cashier says.

"It's all I came for. I was lucky, too — stock boy told me it's the last bottle."

"You really aren't buying anything else? Everyone is leaving with at least a cartful. Usually more."

Wylie shrugs. "I'm already well-stocked. I was before any of this, actually." No beets, though.

She scans them. "I wouldn't say that too loud."

She puts the beets in a plastic bag before he can tell her he doesn't need one. Oh well. He smiles, takes it, and leaves.

Traffic is unusually heavy for the time of day. Everyone's suddenly realized there's some place they desperately need to be. It reminds him of a kicked anthill. He can usually count on Goulds drivers to give him a few breaks on his way out, but not today. Instead, people are making ample use of their horns, and, in one case, even leaning out of windows to exchange obscenities.

This is feeling less and less like Newfoundland.

St. John's is worse. Driving down Queen's Road, he sees a lot of parked cars with tickets fluttering under their wipers. That brings a bitter chuckle. Ever vigilant, the meter maids.

The Rooms parking lot is nearly empty. He goes in and makes his way to the Archives, where Lucy tells him she's the only one working this afternoon. Other than her, and now Wylie, the Archives are empty.

"You're not here to do more research," she says, her eyes a little wider than usual. "Are you, Mr. Ryan?"

Lucy is fresh out of university, by Wylie's guess. She's fairly new. He only learned her name last week.

He shakes his head. "I left my notes here again. Tuesday. They're in a neon green binder."

She reaches under the desk, producing it, but doesn't pass it right away. Instead she hugs the binder against her chest, and for the moment seems to forget she's holding it as she stares into space.

He checks his watch.

"You're the only one I've heard of who's read all our books on the Beothuk cover to cover," she says, still without eye contact. "Twice."

"I like to be thorough."

She looks at him. "I always figured you were writing a thesis or something, but …" She looks away. "I read your notes. Your interest isn't academic, is it?"

"No."

"You saw this coming. Didn't you? The crisis — you've been preparing for it."

"The Beothuks were the last nomadic people to live in Newfoundland. We might need their methods, someday soon."

She gives him the notes. Sitting in his car again, he wants to go home and check on Candy. But more than that, he wants to be done with driving. Permanently, if he can help it. And he has one more stop. So he settles for a text message, and pulls out of the lot.

This morning, Candy woke as he was preparing her insulin shot. She stood on the bottom step, wordless, wearing the same clothes she had on yesterday. She watched him dip a cotton ball in alcohol, roll the insulin bottle between his hands, and sterilize the bottle's rubber lid. He set it on the counter to dry.

"Such a first-world disease," she said.

He looked up. She'd mustered a sad smile.

Before her diagnosis, he rarely called her just Candy. "My Candy Girl," he used to say, or "Sugar Tits," if he was feeling brave. When her doctor told her, he drove straight to the grocery store and bought low-carb noodles for vegetarian diabetic lasagna. "This doesn't have to change much," he said. "You'll see."

Later, in the kitchen, he held out his hand. "Can you pass me the garlic press, Candy Girl?"

Their eyes met. She wasn't smiling, and suddenly, neither was he. That was the last time he called her that.

Red and blue lights flash in his rearview mirror, accompanied by two staccato siren bursts. His heartbeat speeds up. He looks at his speedometer, and his brow furrows.

He hits the power locks.

"Yes?" he says through a two-inch gap between the window and the frame.

"You were speeding."

"I wasn't."

The cop places one hand on the roof of the car and the other on his holster. "You were, actually."

"I was going 50."

"I'm gonna give you a break. I'll only charge you a hundred."

"What? Charge me?"

"Just give me a hundred, and we'll call it even."

"I don't have that."

"Let me see your wallet."

"I won't."

"I'm being polite to you, right now. I don't have to."

"You can write me a ticket, and I'll take it to court and contest it. But what you're attempting here is extortion."

"Court?" The cop laughs. "Do you know Newfoundland only produces 15 per cent of its own food?"

"It's less than that, actually."

The cop smiles. "Exactly. So don't you think we need to start taking the long view?"

"I have. Unfortunately for you, though, the Internet still works." Wylie picks up his smartphone from the passenger seat. "This has been recording our conversation and uploading it to my computer at home. Try anything, and my wife will send the file to your boss. Get your gun taken from you."

"Let me see that."

"Not a chance. Get lost."

He does. Wylie breathes, and rejoins traffic.

He finds the drug store's parking lot filled to capacity and then some, so he parks on the street. Inside, people are milling in and out of the aisles, some with baskets full of over-the-counter drugs and potato chips, others with arms piled high. The lineup to speak with a pharmacist winds around the store.

He spends the next hour watching people scream at the employees and wave their hands. No one seems to meet with much success. When it's his turn he tries to marshal a cheery grin, but the woman behind the counter stares back blank-faced.

"I need to buy some insulin," Wylie says.

"Do you have a prescription?"

"It's run out. But —"

"I'm sorry, sir. Until we're able to receive new shipments, we have strict instructions not to sell medicine to anyone without a prescription."

"There won't be any new shipments. The economy's crashed. Oil prices are never coming back down."

"Don't raise your voice to me, sir."

"Please. My wife's supply will only last two weeks more."

"I suggest your wife make an appointment with her doctor."

"She can't get in to see her doctor. He's completely booked, just like every other doctor in town."

"This is the new policy. There's nothing I can do."

Wylie leaves the pharmacy and walks to his car, feeling numb. He reaches for the door handle, but pauses, and goes to the trunk instead. He pops it. There's a small metal shovel kept here, for emergencies.

He takes it out. Tests the weight of it in his hands.

There will be blood, soon. He knows it. St. John's will run red.

But he puts the shovel back in the trunk, and drives home.

•••

SCOTT BARTLETT *was born 1987, in St. John's. He's been writing fiction since he was 15. His second novel, "Royal Flush," received the H.R. (Bill) Percy Prize, and his third novel, "Taking Stock," received the Lawrence Jackson Award and the Percy Janes First Novel Award.*

Reconciliation

By Mary Pike

"Sir, Mrs. Murphy wants some coal."

Mr. Rossiter nodded and stepped from behind his desk. His footsteps echoed as he slow-paced the aisles of his multi-grade classroom. With his wooden pointer he tapped a dog-eared "King Arthur for Boys" half hidden under Jake's arithmetic book, and rapped Eli's desk. "You two. Make yourselves useful."

The third-graders hopped up. "Yes, sir!" They swaggered toward the back of the classroom.

Jake touched the trapdoor first. He grabbed the handle set into the wooden floor and heaved back the hatch. His voice dropped on octave. "I'm going down." He squared his shoulders.

Eli swung the coal scuttle toward Jake. "Remember that joke about the naked lady and the coal merchant?"

Jake nodded.

"So, hard or soft?"

"Shhh, b'y. Don't let Old Baldy hear you!"

On cue, Mr. Rossiter called from his dais. "Boys! The soft coal is in the left bin and the hard in the right. Mrs. Murphy wants some hard."

The boys giggled.

Jake navigated four wooden steps into the darkness. He felt the air for a dangling string and pulled. A low wattage bulb illuminated the dirt cellar. Coal dust swirled and settled as he shoveled.

"Done," he called.

Eli bent and grabbed the scuttle's handle with both hands. He grunted and squinted his eyes shut. The full bucket inched upwards.

An arm emerged from the darkness. Jake grabbed Eli's crotch. Eli squealed and the coal bucket crashed through the hole.

"Jakie's dead!" screamed the girls.

Mr. Rossiter pushed through the students. Mrs. Murphy barged in. "Clear a path," he yelled to her. "I have a casualty to take to the hospital."

At the General, the doctor ambled up to the chain-smoking teacher.

"A nasty bump," he said, "but the boy will be all right." He waved a sheaf of papers. "I have to write a report."

Mr. Rossiter concluded with, "I was reminded of when the hand rose from the lake for King Arthur's sword."

The doctor's chuckles followed Mr. Rossiter and a sniveling Jake out to the teacher's Land Rover. Coal dust blanketed the child's hair and face, his checkered shirt and patched pants. It clung to the tip of a toe poking through a cracked canvas shoe. On Military Road, Mr. Rossiter stopped at Noseworthy's. He emerged with a root beer and a Superman comic. He placed both in Jake's lap.

Mr. Rossiter parked outside a Georgetown row house stippled with whitewash. Mrs. Snow rushed out, trailing the stale odour of fried fish. "I heard you was near killed," she cried. She gathered Jake to her, and then pushed him away. "How could you grab poor Eli like that?" She cuffed her son and pushed him through the front door. "He's been nothing but trouble since his poor father drownded, God rest his soul," she said. "I'm doing me best, what with the baby and taking in boarders. But all he does is sits like a fool and reads." Mrs. Snow blanched. "Pardon me words, sir, but education isn't for the likes of us." She fingered diaper pins dangling from her cotton dress. "Now, you have to punish him for what he done to poor Eli."

"That crawlin' squid. That dogfish." Jake leaned on his shovel and hawked black spit into the dirt. He eyed the mound of coal remaining in front of Mr. Rossiter's, and a bigger mound by a neighbour's cellar chute. He knuckled the corners of his eyes and streaked wet grime from his eyes to his ears. "If it's the last thing I do …" He punctuated each word with a shovelful of coal, "I'll … get … him!"

"Hey, Jake!" Eli marched up, shovel in hand. "I didn't mean to get you into trouble, b'y." He tackled the pile of coal.

Mr. Rossiter formed a Worm Digging Committee and promised a penny for each can of worms.

Jake and Eli dug in Mr. Mullet's vegetable garden because he squinted with nearsightedness and walked with a cane.

"I'm keeping the fat ones." Jake held up a wriggler. "They might have babies."

"Where you going to keep 'em?"

"Dunno, yet." He gathered some dirt and pocketed both.

A kitchen curtain fell back into place.

A sharp knocking drew Mrs. Snow to her door. Mr. Mullet brandished his cane and shook Jake like he was shaking dirt off a carrot.

"You've got to beat him," he said.

"Why?"

"He's digging in me garden."

"Boys do that."

"Y-y-you b-b-beat him! He p-p-p-issed in me well, too!"

"I won't beat him, he never p-p-p-issed in mine!"

Mrs. Snow grabbed Jake's shirt and pulled him into their home. She slammed her door on the local bootlegger.

"What's all this about?"

"Me and Eli was only digging for worms."

"And pissing in wells! Get the strap."

An aching Jake stole through his house after midnight. In the parlour he gently deposited five fat worms in his mother's prized pot of lilies. "That shagger. Him and his stupid committee."

Jake made the rules of Sheep simple: he was in charge.

"Baaa," he bleated. "Baaa.

"Maaa," answered the others. They crawled through a field on grass-stained knees.

"Baa … Christ Almighty!"

Jake jumped up and ran with the others close behind. They jostled under a streetlight to see the oozing blood.

There was no blood.

Only a brown, dog-turd hand.

Jake stared. Transfixed.

"By the jeezly Christ," he muttered.

"Baaa!" Jake yelled and sprinted out of the field and down Barnes Road.

"Maaa!" The others followed full pelt.

"Baaa!"

"Maaa!"

Jake cut into Bulger's Lane and flew past the old forge. On McDougall Street he leapfrogged a concrete hopper. The boys followed suit. They ran flat out and pulled up short in front of Mr. Rossiter's home. Jake crept forward. Slowly, almost lovingly, he worked his brown hand over the doorknob's pitted surface. He smiled and stepped back. "That'll fix the bastard."

The boys darted to a nearby laneway. They sucked in their breaths when Mr. Rossiter stepped into view. Old Baldy sniffed, lifting and examining the bottom of each shoe.

He reached for the doorknob.

Jake and Eli threw themselves into the Capitol Theatre's plush seats. In the matinee confusion, the nine-year-olds struck a match and puffed like steamer smokestacks on butts they'd picked up.

The projector clattered.

The children roared when gap-toothed Long John Silver appeared. Alongside fighting pirates they unsheathed imaginary cutlasses and brandished them in the air.

A thoughtful Mr. Rossiter strolled home after the movie. Early the next morning he placed a book in Jake's desk.

Jake left school alone. Guilt niggled. From under his jacket he drew out the prized "Treasure Island." He fingered the book and thought about his Superman comic. His stomach lurched.

All night Jake tossed and turned. At daybreak he tiptoed to the parlour. He dug nine worms from the flowerpot before bedsprings creaked upstairs. He dropped the worms into a paper bag and scooted out the back door. Between his house and Mr. Rossiter's he grabbed a few handfuls of dirt. For the second time in a week he approached his teacher's front door.

On the top step, Jake left his amends.

•••

MARY PIKE *is an award-winning author of both fiction and nonfiction. She is a St. John's native with stories published in "The Cuffer Anthology Volumes II, III, IV and V."*

Sculpins

By Dara Squires

"You won't catch nothing like that," some gnarled old man yells as I dangle my bare hook off the tarry wharf.

"Sculpins ain't nothing," I sauce back at him. Mind your own business, you bag of rotten tobacco.

"That's where you're wrong," he laughs back, shaking his head.

I knows what he thinks, that I'm some dumb townie. I don't care. He can think what he wants. I wants to catch a sculpin to gross out Prissy Chrissy. Last time I was here she called me a tomboy, which I don't mind, really, except she said it with a sneer. And I minds a sneer.

I'd rather be catching sculpins in my grubby old shorts than prancing around in a skirt afraid to drink from the hose cause I might mess my lipstick, like her.

I like to catch 'em and show 'em to her and dare her to take 'em off the hook. She squeals, "You can't touch 'em, you'll get some skin disease!" So I kicks 'em off with my foot and then I lift up their torn old bloody bodies to show her before I throw 'em back under the wharf.

This wharf is where I learned to swim. "Sink or swim," my dad said, and threw me off. I weren't scared at all, even though I swallowed some nasty salt water that puckered my throat closed. I was fine till I thought of the sculpins under the wharf and how they might be mad at me for killing their brothers and sisters and stuff.

Be horrible to be drowned by a mob of angry sculpins. That's what I told him when he pulled me out. I sputtered and smacked him 'cross the face for scaring me like that. I got bent over his knee for that one, but it was worth it.

All them rotten sculpin bodies under there do give me the willies though. So now when I dives off I make sure to jump good and wide from the wharf. Prissy Chrissy climbs down the ladder and squeals about the eel grass.

Sometimes I sink right down into it and wrap it 'round myself and pretend I'm caught and drowning. Then I struggle and fight till I get free and zoom up to the surface. No one notices though. The boys think I'm just a girl and the girls think if I ain't interested in their candy store lipstick then I'm no good anyway. Just like a sculpin.

Prissy Chrissy likes my brother, which is wrong cause they're cousins. Kissin' cousins make funny babies, that's what my uncle always says. There's a family down the shore with three weird kids, big drooly lumps that laugh when you say hello and laugh when you say goodbye and just shake their heads around in between. Their parents are cousins, my mother says, and that's why they're like that.

Would serve Prissy Chrissy right to have a kid like that. Be some hard to be all proper and perfect with a snot-nosed 10 year old drooling and shitting all over you. Can just see her trying to drag him off to Sunday school now, with him yelling out curse words and shaking the spit right out of his mouth.

When she likes a boy she stands around a lot with her friends and laughs. I saw her doin' it last year with Rotten John. Her and her girlfriends put on their swimsuits and then don't even swim. They just stand around chewing gum and laughing. And making fun of me so the boys'll notice them. Before they started in on that tomboy crap the boys always let me horse around with them. But now it's like they're afraid I'm going to grow tits and get silly like her.

I told her her laugh sounded some tinkly and sweet, just like the sound of piss hitting a toilet. Then she snuck off and flattened my bike tires while I was swimming.

Brave, she's not. I've a mind to put a sculpin in her bed. Smear it all over her sheets so she'll get it all over her skin and get sculpin leprosy. She'd look some funny with her nose rotting and falling off right above her wild cherry lipstick and under her blue lagoon eyeshadow.

I think they names crayons better than makeup. That's for sure. But she calls me a baby when I say things like that.

I hates spending the summer here but Dad says I got to on account of Mom not liking me too much. He doesn't say it like that, but I knows that's what he means. I give her breakdowns, like that crap Ford we used to own.

I never asked to be born. That's what I say. Sometimes I yells it at them. The two of 'em. When they're fighting about me. Mom wants to send me away to live with her sister. 'Cause she's got two girls and they're supposed to be good for me. Away on the mainland where I won't be under bad influences. Like mainlanders ain't bad influences. Everyone says they're the worst sort.

I knows she just wants to be rid of me. My brothers can take care of themselves but sometimes I needs her to read my stuff from school or brush my hair when it's all tangles. She hates that. She grabs my arm and twists it hard to hold me still while she rips at my hair. I think I'd rather have tangles. But Miss at school says I can't have tangles and I gotta wear clean clothes and brush my teeth and wash my hands after I takes a piss.

I don't know why it matters so much to her anyway. Ain't her hair that's gonna get lousy if it ain't washed. But I like to make Miss happy, all the same, even though she says there's no hope for me. She smells nice and when she wears a skirt she doesn't prance around like Chrissy. She just stands there. Reminds me of the horse our neighbour has. Standing fine in a field.

Miss says that parents aren't supposed to hurt their kids or yell at them or nothing like that. Miss is strange. I think she might be a mainlander, really, 'cause she talks right proper.

She gave me a book at the end of the year. She says that by the end of the summer I oughta be able to read it. Chrissy says I'm a baby for not being able to read but it's some hard to learn the words if no one will read it to you.

I keep it under my bed and when Chrissy gets to be so much for me I wants to fling sculpins and eel grass in everyone's faces, I slides in under the bed with my book and a flashlight. It's quiet and dark in there, like under the wharf. I lie there reading, just an angry, thrown-away sculpin, trying to figure out them words.

I think if someone dangled a hook down to me I might just bite it too, just cause I knows they wants me to. Be nice to be wanted.

•••

DARA SQUIRES is a social media specialist with Best Boy Entertainment. An award-winning writer and parenting columnist, she writes in the midst of wrangling three kids and pouring more coffee. She has bright red hair.

Cat's Paw

By Harold N. Walters

"It's for your own good, Pepper," said Festus.

Then he brought down the axe.

Two weeks earlier, Pepper, Festus' valiant black and grey she-cat fought a lynx in the woods behind the barn. Fought and lost.

Festus had heard cats yowling in the night but had paid it no mind; cats by their nocturnal nature prowl and howl in the night.

Next morning he found Pepper lying wounded on the porch. Her face and body were raked by long scratches, none of which appeared to be killers, not at a glance anyway. Pepper's left front paw showed the most serious injury. It was mangled as if its bones had been chewed bloody.

"Reckon you run into a lynx or a damn big tom," Festus said while kneeling to examine Pepper's wounds.

Lifting her gently and trying to ignore her piteous maroawing, Festus carried Pepper to the barn and fixed her a bed on a sack of hay.

Because Festus lived in a time and place where folks mostly administered to their ailing animals as best they could manage, he settled her as comfortably as he could and left to fetch some things to tend her injuries.

Festus returned with liniments, ointments and bandage cloths he had sterilized on the stovetop. Despite Pepper's moaning, throaty growl, he doctored her damaged paw and wrapped it with the scorched gauze and cotton.

"It's not looking good, Pepper," he said. "We can only hope for the best."

The next day when he peeled the bandage from Pepper's wound Festus grimaced and reflexively turned his head aside from the foul smell rising from the cat's festering paw.

"Phew," he said, then swabbed the wound clean, applied fresh unguents and fastened a new dressing.

Pepper offered a feeble mew.

Festus left Pepper with a bowl of watery milk into which he had stirred some alcohol-laced tonic on the off chance that it would be of some medicinal value.

"I'll have another look at it tomorrow," he said and left, praying Pepper was tough enough to fight off the infection.

Daily, Pepper's paw worsened, despite Festus' regular attention. And daily through the slits of her feverish eyes Pepper watched Festus clean and wrap her paw.

Even though she lapped feebly at the saucer of milk she lost weight; her body pined away.

At the beginning of Pepper's second week of misery Festus feared there was no hope for her recovery. Increased swelling in the mauled paw led Festus to believe blood poisoning was likely to spread up her leg. The still weeping wound continued to stink of putrefying flesh.

"Gangrene, I reckon." Festus whispered as if Pepper knew the meaning of the word.

By the end of the week, Festus knew he must decide Pepper's fate. Would he continue to nurse the sick cat, or, as much as he hated to see the suffering cat dead, put her out of her misery?

Traditionally, folks in Pelican Cove simply drowned unwanted cats. Yet Festus smote his forehead as if thumping his brain to discover a better means of dispatching Pepper.

He sat on the hay beside Pepper, gently scratching between her ears as he had so often done when she jumped into his lap while he savoured his after-supper smoke.

Through the barn's opened door Festus could look across his yard to his woodpile and see his heaviest wood-cleaving axe wedged, like the gnomon of a sundial, deep into the top of the stump he used as a chopping block. Beyond the woodpile he saw the bucket of pitch he had recently used to patch a leak in his woodshed's roof.

After studying and sorting his thoughts, Festus sighed.

"That might actually work, Pepper," he said. "It's certainly worth a try."

Hauling himself to his feet, Festus left Pepper's sick bed, strode across the yard, hoisted the pitch bucket and entered the woodshed.

Soon the hiss of a blowtorch filled the woodshed.

When Festus stepped back outside carrying the bucket of pitch, he wore a pair of thick leather gloves, ones he used to protect his hands when working with extremely hot liquids like the molten lead he sometimes used to seal cast iron pipes — or to handle heated tar.

He set the steaming bucket of pitch on the ground to the left of his chopping block.

He wiggled the axe loose and lodged it flat on top of the block.

Turning, he headed for the barn.

Inside the barn, Festus lifted Pepper and cradled her as carefully as he could in the palms of the heavy gloves.

Grimly, he set out for the chopping block.

Within a minute, because imminent harshness, like lancing a boil with one smooth scalpel stroke, should be swift, Festus said, "It's for your own good, Pepper."

Then he brought down the axe.

At noon of a sunny day almost four weeks after Pepper fought the lynx, Festus stood spraddle-legged at his chopping block splitting large junks of birch as he had been doing all morning. No evidence of Pepper's blood remained in the diced top of the block.

Festus whistled while he worked. Sweat darkened his hatband.

Resting in the shade beneath the woodshed's eave, Pepper licked at the remaining scabs of tar that Festus had used to cauterize and seal the stump of her leg a split second after he had brought down the axe.

Pepper watched Festus intently, her face as inscrutable as the face of an Egyptian cat idol; as inscrutable as the face of a Nubian queen watching a toiling slave who had violated her body to save her life.

• • •

HAROLD N. WALTERS, *a self-proclaimed veritable dinosaur, lives happily ever after in Dunville. He is tickled to dwell in Newfoundland, the only Canadian province with its own time zone. How cool is that?*

Fire Balloon

By Scott Bartlett

Most of Michael's life was dim to him, now. That happens after 91 years. He remembered shades of happiness, and plenty of sad hues, too. Blurred faces, people who had jostled him one way or another. Car trips. Back and forth across the island, endlessly.

The clearest memories were of his progeny. Michael had worked in a darkroom since he was 14, and both his children and their children had joined him there in their youth, for long hours filled with fascination. None had followed in his footsteps — thank God. Digital photography killed his old profession as surely as video had done for radio stars.

His grandchildren were mostly grown now, and when his sickness came, he welcomed it. He didn't have a death wish. But he was 91, for Christ's sake, and the world looked bleak to him, in spite of the fancy phones they all carried.

His children wanted him to be in St. John's, which was where most of them had migrated. He consented. He would end up wherever God put him, no matter his point of departure.

Two weeks later, they were all gathered around his hospital bed, taking turns holding his hands. In his delirium he turned to his only daughter, Esther, who'd hewn closest to the old beliefs.

"Have I been good?"

She patted his hand and nodded, her eyes moist. She paused, and nodded again.

He drifted away.

• • •

Bright, white light.

He tried to open his eyes, and couldn't.

"Where am I?" he rasped.

Clothes rustled, to his left. A hand gripped his knee.

"You're in ICU, Dad. With us." Luke. "You're still with us."

This time, he opened his eyes.

"How?"

"A new procedure. Experimental. They said it was your only chance — slim, but we figured you'd want to take it."

"You brats," Michael said, and pain in his chest made him pause. "You brats don't get your inheritance yet."

Stephen chuckled. "That's a shame. I've had my eye on that ratty old sofa."

• • •

Stephen's orphans were sending fire balloons out over the lake.

Well, they weren't technically orphans. Their mother was still alive somewhere, presumably. She'd disappeared shortly after Stephen's cancer diagnosis, and hadn't checked in with anyone since.

Stephen's oldest, Samuel, picked up another balloon and lit the alcohol-soaked cotton ball sitting in its basket. He gave it to his brother Daniel to release.

Daniel watched it go, rapt. "Do you think it will float on forever?"

"No," Samuel said. "That's stupid."

Luke pulled up in his DeLorean. He walked over, hand extended. His smile wavered, and after a couple seconds he put his hand in his pocket.

"Happy birthday, Dad."

Michael said nothing.

Luke cleared his throat, and sat next to him on the picnic table. "Fire balloons," he said, nodding at the children. "Ray Bradbury would be proud."

"Who?"

"Never mind." Luke twisted around and grabbed a fistful of chips from one of the bowls on the table. "So," he said through a mouthful. "Triple digits today, hey? Hope that happens to me."

"Your mother used to say neither of us would last long, without the other."

Luke stopped chewing for a moment.

"I guess she was wrong," Michael said.

Daniel ran up with his gadget and pointed the screen at him. "Check out my new app, Pop! It's a pet you can really feed, and everything!"

Michael grunted, and looked away.

"Show me, Danny," Luke said. "Poppy's not into that stuff." Danny passed him the phone. "Hey, cool! A guy had this at Sci-Fi on the Rock this year. You might actually get a kick out of this, Dad. It uses the phone's camera to make it look like there's really a little critter running around. It eats imaginary food and craps imaginary crap. It's the kind of pet you might have actually let us have when we were kids."

Luke held the screen in front of him. It showed what looked like cotton candy with eyes rolling about on the grass.

Michael picked up his cane and, with great effort, got to his feet. He looked at his son. "And you wonder why you've never had a girlfriend."

Luke stood and followed him as he hobbled toward the house. The door opened before they reached the porch. It was Esther, her eyes rimmed with red, as they always were of late. She had found a new therapist.

They sat together on hard plastic chairs.

"Dad," Luke said, "have you given any more thought—"

"No. And I won't."

Everyone else was dead who'd had the same procedure Michael did. Now the doctors wanted to preserve him in an ice box for future study. An old man, well past his time. Ludicrous.

"The technology for cryopreservation is there now, Dad, and almost nobody gets this opportunity. You could live to see—"

"I've seen it all."

"But—"

"He doesn't want it, Luke," Esther said, her voice ragged. "Can't you see that?"

...

The sun was an angry blister on the day the young man came for Michael. The man had been wiping sweat from his brow with the back of his hand for as long as they'd been arguing.

"Sir," he said, "this is no longer a choice. As I'm sure you know, under new Canadian law, certain personal rights are suspended if it is deemed beneficial to the Canadian people. Now, are you going to put up resistance? Do I have to restrain you?"

Michael could do nothing, of course. The man gripped him by the upper arm and escorted him to a waiting car, helping him into the back.

"Hi, Dad."

It was Luke.

Michael stared. "Why are you with them?"

Luke put a hand on Michael's knee. "They're preserving me, too."

"Why?"

"I can afford it."

"You want this?"

Luke smiled. "This is how it begins, Dad. This is the first taste of immortality."

"What are you talking about?"

"Well, I know you don't care for quantum physics—" Luke paused, and a little laugh escaped his lips. "But try to follow along. If you consider the implications of multiverse theory, taken with quantum theory, you realize no one ever actually dies. You see, for a quantum event to be resolved, there must be an observer, and you can't observe your own death. So every time an event occurs that might have caused you to die, multiple universes are created, and you'll always end up in one where you survive."

Michael looked out the window. "Right."

Esther was waiting in the room where they would freeze him. They put him in a wheelchair, and he looked up at her.

"I'm sorry, Esther," he said. "I should have listened."

"I forgive you."

But he knew she didn't.

She'd tried to tell him, many times. And the day Michael walked in on his brother with eight-year-old Esther, he beat him till his face was a bloody ruin.

But the damage had been done.

...

Many decades later, he woke to robotic arms wielding hot sponges.

"Your son didn't keep," a voice said from an intercom. "Sorry."

Michael knew then that Esther had lied: he hadn't been good.

He hadn't been good after all.

∴

SCOTT BARTLETT *was born 1987, in St. John's. He's been writing fiction since he was 15. His second novel, "Royal Flush," received the H.R. (Bill) Percy Prize, and his third novel, "Taking Stock," received the Lawrence Jackson Award and the Percy Janes First Novel Award.*

Gum

By Melanie Oates

I stood under the streetlight clutchin myself, waitin for the bus. Buses in St. John's are rarely on time. The fall air sizzled my face as the throbbin lights of the hospital across the street lured me into a trance. Worn-out nurses shovin pills down their patients' gobs and treatin the ailment, not the person. It was just after supper hour. I thought of an old man, his belly full of lukewarm hospital gruel, entertainin visitors who came out of obligation.

The drama department of the university was puttin off a production of some local play. I bought a ticket, hopped on the bus and went. Since movin to the city I hadn't really kept in touch with any of my high school friends, though I don't know if that would be the fittin term for many of them. They all went to be teachers or secretaries or engineers, to wear their stilettos and matchin outfits when they scheduled a Girl's Night Out, to get drunk enough to giggle about the ways they let their boyfriends at 'em sometimes. For some reason I thought of myself as different from them, but really, I was studyin to be a biologist. I worked it around inside myself until it felt different, anyway. I started busing around to things by myself.

I waited for my ticket in the great oak lobby of the Arts Building with its portraits of mustached men and golden engraved plaques. A girl about my age came out from behind a forbidden door. She had this long curly hair and she was the kind of pretty that everybody could agree on. She was wearin a thick green wool jacket. She was in the play. My eyes stalked her as she spoke to this man, dressed all in black. Whatever he said must have been funny cause her head collapsed back, the hair wrigglin down her shoulders when she laughed. To be her.

I was next in line and handed my ticket to the students, also dressed in black. They passed me a photocopied black and white program. Enjoy the show, they said in unison, wrinklin up their faces with phony smiles. Even to be them.

A while back I overheard a prof makin a big deal out of the guy who wrote the play, so I'd been readin his work and he wasn't half-bad. I had a quick gull-look around but I wouldn't have known him anyway. <u>How it must feel to have somethin that you spent so much time with alone given a heartbeat right in front of you.</u> Him, he was the one to be.

The theatre was back-alley black. We were taken onto the stage where foldout chairs were divided in two long rows, two seats wide with a narrow walkway in between. We were on a bus. I took a seat at the front. I heard a couple behind me giggle as they sat. "You can have the window seat," the young fella said to the girl. Spitballs and paper airplanes with pointed tips on 'em like darts whipped through by mind. The seat beside me stayed empty.

A blue spotlight popped on right in front of me to reveal a young fella hung across a bench, jackshirt and jeans, half-conscious, with a seepin lip. The girl from earlier entered and slid in beside him. They were on the bus, too. It turned out the man couldn't remember anything, even the girl. I watched, totally lost and forgettin myself, until the girl spoke to the bloodied-up man and she was me:

"What do you think you know about me? From what you can see and suppose, I mean. You can probably see a lot.

"That I'm dressed well, but my clothes aren't too precious, they've been worn, so likely I grew up in a middle-class family.

"That my home life was pretty good — but a lot of things were kept under wraps.

"That I didn't have to work very hard to do well in school because I'm smart and I know it.

"That I'm average weight and average height but I hate the word average.

"That I try to be good but have had many moments of bad — especially during times when I've felt ugly.

"That I've had my slutty moments, only some of which I regret.

"That I have screwed up, but I'm not a screw-up.

"That I don't mind saying these things because I know nobody can judge me quite like I judge myself.

"That I think the colour green looks good on me.

"That I ride the bus."

I was her. But she was not me, no. She was an actress playin me and I couldn't believe that any of those things could be true of her. Well, maybe green did look good on her. After that I wasn't in it. I was me watchin her, as her and not as the character she was playin, and I hated her for knowin all of those secrets about me, for sayin them out loud and for pretendin that she knew how it felt.

As I ran down over the stairs to the exit I heard her voice call out to him, "What did you think? Did we do your words justice?" I couldn't even turn around to see what he looked like, the playwright.

The bus was surreal then, like I was in the play. But there was no dramatic lighting or cute troubled man. Instead, a hugely overweight elderly woman with a cane sat beside me. People on buses have no eyes or presence. There is little chatter and many headphones. That's why when I started to cry right there I didn't mind. It was the same as if I'd just got the hiccups. Nobody could see me. I wasn't that actress or even that flashlight boy, and I would never be that playwright.

The hell hearse stopped about a one-minute walk from where it had just picked us up and the old lady got off. I had relaxed onto the second seat but had to squash into the window again when a grey-haired man sat next to me. He tapped his leg in time with the music that I could hear through his headphones. I pointed my singed eyes out the grubby window. The man unplugged one of his ears.

"Are you OK?"

It was like he Tasered me. He'd stunned my vocabulary.

"Gum?"

He held out a yellow package filled with tinfoil-wrapped sticks.

I took one. Chewed.

We rode wordless until my stop. He got up to let me out, which not everybody does, let me tell ya.

"Thanks again for the gum."

"You're welcome. Feel better."

It wasn't until a week later when I got over the trauma of seein myself on stage that I was able to look at the program. On the back page, smilin over the top of his glasses, there he was.

・・・

MELANIE OATES *is a writer who received the 2010 Percy Janes First Novel Award, is a recent MUN graduate, and though she grew up on the Southern Shore, is now a bit of a townie.*

Heart of the Matter

By Jacquie S. Fleming

He grabbed her arm as she passed him in the hallway, pulling Sara against his chest. Close enough she could smell the warmth of his leather jacket. Close enough she could taste the last cigarette he'd smoked.

"Meet me at the car after school. You can watch me shoot bottles down by the beach." He kissed her neck, his breath lingering on her skin. He walked away, laughing to himself.

Vaughan drove with one arm draped over the steering wheel and the other resting on the gearshift. He grabbed her hand and smiled. "Have you ever shot a gun?" he asked.

Sara shook her head. "No, I've watched my cousins do it sometimes." His right hand moved to her knee.

He set up four beer bottles on a rock outcropping that fingered itself into the cold grey water. It was littered with little mounds of broken glass glinting in the sun. The water lapped the shoreline, gently rolling pebbles, shells and pieces of glass, reshaping them against the sand.

He unwrapped the gun from a blanket. It looked so real. Not like those her cousins used that spurted out green plastic pellets that could down a robin or shoot someone's eye out. "Nice hey?" said Vaughan.

Sara nodded. "That doesn't look like any BB gun I've ever seen."

"That's because it's not a BB gun. It's a .22. The real thing. Bolt action, 5 shot." He lifted the rifle to his shoulder. Pursing his lips, he blew her a kiss and then slid his gaze back to his target. He shifted a metal lever. Vaughan gently squeezed the trigger.

Crack!

A bottle exploded, shards bursting out in all directions.

Another lever shift. Ping. Metal against metal.

Crack!

Another bottle blasted apart. Shift. Ping. Squeeze. Crack! And again.

Four shots. Four beer bottles reduced to shards. Sara's leaden feet refused to move. The smell of burning surrounded her. Gunpowder? Fear.

Vaughan cradled the rifle under his arm while he reached down into the cardboard box. He pulled out something red and tossed it to Sara. An apple. She could smell its crisp sweetness.

"Hold that flat on your palm and stretch your arm out to the side. Keep still." Vaughan said. He wasn't smiling anymore. "Do it." The gun was pointed straight at her. She hesitated for a moment. "Now," he said.

Sara balanced the apple on her hand, slid her arm out and closed her eyes. She heard the metal shift and sensed his aim.

Crack!

The apple tumbled from her hand, hitting the sand. Sara dropped to her knees, unable to breathe, bile rising in her throat. She could smell cooked apple. Like applesauce or apple pie, no cinnamon. Opening her eyes she saw the red apple beside her, intact. Still in one piece. Except for a hole running through its core, its heart.

She heard Vaughan speak. "Trust me, Sara?"

Sara sobbed. She had loved Vaughan once, loved everything about him. Until today.

...

JACQUIE S. FLEMING *writes short stories, a little poetry and teaches creative writing for children. She sees a story embedded in everything and uses it to her advantage.*

Killing With Kindness

By Dolores Hynes

There he is all laid out in his Sunday best. JimJoe never looked so good, they said, all dolled up, all dickied off. Gommel. Good as gold, they said, would give you the shirt off his back. It wouldn't be his own shirt, I wanted to say, but what odds, he's just where I want him, tucked in right snug in the pale green satin.

Life is queer, they said, another few days to your anniversary — 40 years is a long time. And don't I know it. I have no worries about going to hell because I've been in and out of hell a lifetime. And how good were you to him — the scoffs you cooked up, all hours of the night and day. Lately, he's been bustin' at the seams.

Yes, ma'am, bustin' is the word. According to the autopsy report, JimJoe's heart exploded, and when they took one look at the rock-hard arteries, they sewed him up right quick. No questions asked. The doctor signed the report and, whoosh, away he'll go, under the sod in the morning. No need to worry about his stomach contents being discovered — a fine-sized pan of sausages, a plate of scrunchions and flat chips, a loaf of homemade bread and butter and a whole lemon meringue pie — I'm a free woman.

When the hospital called I knew I was holding a trump card, and it didn't take me long to decide how to play it. All winter long, JimJoe had been scraping the bottom of the pity barrel. He romanced about the pain in his back and his jaw and his head, and said he felt so logy he could barely drag himself up to the club. When someone in the harbour had a complaint, Mr. Misery would have the same thing. Proper circus. When I'd tell him the only sickness he had was known as pure idleness, the racket would start. And he could be vicious.

Well, after our last big row, he took off for the club, half cut, all riled up, got the boss goin'-over, ended up out in Emergency, and, between the jigs and the reels, had a blood test. I was hoping they'd keep him in, so's I could get a bit of peace, but the Lord works in mysterious ways. Shortage of beds, they said, better off home. But JimJoe wasn't home three hours when the freedom call came and, as luck would have it, His Lordship was out in the shed drinking beer.

According to the bearer of the good news, his blood pressure was to the rafters, as were his cholesterol and blood sugar, and if my man didn't soon get help, he could be dead in six weeks. I can't explain the warm feeling that trickled over me. Six weeks. The angelic voice was telling me that JimJoe had to give up the booze, the fats and the sweets, get off the daybed and try to stay calm. He'd be calm all right.

As I was hanging up, JimJoe appeared in the door demanding to know who I was talking to. Right jealous he was. He nearly fell down in a pile when I put my arms around him, telling him the hospital called to say his constitution was weak and needed to be built up, and that I was going to make him feel like he'd never felt before. I started in right there and then catering to most of Prince Charming's whims and fancies. He couldn't believe his new position of importance.

His hag of a mother came over that night when I was frying up a pan of black puddings. Marvelling at the sudden change in me she was, saying it was about time I realized how cushy I had it, that JimJoe's bark was worse than his bite. I felt like showing her the print of his canines in my arm, but for the sake of six weeks, I thought, shag it, and agreed with her. She seemed stunned for a second, but then started accusing me of winning the lottery. I laughed and offered her a pudding.

The next morning I hightailed it over to the shop with my list of medicines. I had to have the basics — salt beef, salt pork, bacon, ham, tins of Klik and Kam, margarine, sugar and a few packs of Flaky buns. Of course, Newsy Hole there had to wonder what was going on. I didn't gratify her with an answer, took a case of Black Horse from the cooler and told her to mark the works down to JimJoe.

I have to say I took great pleasure in watching himself lap the big, greasy feeds aboard of him. I made sure he drank the pot liquor off the beef and cabbage; once, I even patted the grizzle off his double chin. Imagining that the daily entrées of rashers were scalding the guts out of him cheered me up, and knowing that the fat would be curdling his blood kept me going. The extra salt on his eggs and baloney would drive his blood pressure to the blue blazes, and I'd have to give him something strong, like a double Morgan and Coke, for the headache. I knew that killing the lout with kindness was the perfect plan the morning he downed the four plates of toutons and molasses and then declared he had to go back to bed.

Now, I never said my plan was easy; it's some hard to smile and tend on someone when you can't stand the sight of him. And cooking three heavy meals, along with the mug ups, takes up your day and is far from cheap. I thought about mixing a bit of antifreeze with his drink, or shoving him down the cellar stairs when he was half in the bag (just to hurry things along) but the risk of getting caught wasn't worth it. A scattered time I'd be overcome with guilt, but then I'd see the smug look on ol' Saucy Puss as I lugged in boughs for the fire and all feelings of remorse would vanish. The odd time, I'd wonder if the blood test missus called about was really his, but I certainly wasn't making any inquiries. I decided to "focus on my goal," like they say on the weight-loss programs; in six weeks I'd have dropped over 300 pounds.

So there you have it. The For Sale sign is done up. Dodge Ram, Big Red and Ski-Doo, along with Ms. Shed and all her belongings should tide me over for a while, at least until the black hat days have run their course. The official mourners are telling me that I'm like someone in the dawnies, and that I should take a spell. I'll rest tomorrow when Bucko there is six feet under. Right now, I have to pick out one last hymn; "Mine Eyes Have Seen the Glory" is a dandy.

•••

DOLORES HYNES *likes to write, stories, songs and skits. She loves Newfoundland and Labrador-inspired material. Her story, "The Hole and the Jam Jams," was published in "Stories from the Hole in the Ceiling" by Anne Galway. Hynes is also the author of song, "Woman of the Island."*

Lady Slipper

By Paul Whittle

— *"This is a classic example of a wild flower that defies domestication. It seems to grow in specific sites and cannot tolerate any environmental changes."*

"Already cremated? Why didn't you wait?" Ann said to her mother on her cell as she neared the airport. She was watching backhoes, ones just like her old man had used, busy removing the edible world like T-Rexes, gnawing foliage to make room for larger monsters: homes and strip malls.

"There was no point in waiting, I was just doing what yer father said. I told you what he wanted. I mean 'is not as if he would have had to greet a half a dozen mourners. You can help scatter his ashes with me," Doris said.

"But God, I'm on my way now… we're almost at the airport. I'll be there tomorrow afternoon by the time we drive up the coast. You couldn't have waited?"

"You couldn't have come sooner?"

Ann put the phone down in her lap so her mother couldn't hear.

"Christ," she said. Then put the phone to her ear again.

"OK, how are you holding up?"

"Fine. It's a relief the suffering is finally over. Anyway, I'm getting a dog."

"What? OK, Mom. Where are you?"

"I just pulled in the driveway. I had the urn strapped in the passenger seat, but the seatbelt indicator was driving me nuts. I wouldn't want him rolling around on the floor."

"So what did you do?"

"He's between my legs."

"Oh Mom, you think that's funny. Would you want someone doing that to you?"

"He's smiling down on us I'm sure right now, wherever he is."

"Have you been drinking?"

"I just stopped in for a few drinks with the girls from the plant on the way home."

"And you left the urn in the car?"

"Well, I have some respect. I wouldn't leave him in the car."

"God, mother."

"Just being practical. He would like that. We'll have people over for drinks when you come. You know, the b'ys he hunted with; it's what he wanted."

No matter how many times she'd taken the final flight from somewhere on the mainland into Deer Lake, she was still fascinated by the subtle changes in both the people and the landscape of the island. Stout men coming back from working time away became more sanguine as they approached home, and yet looking down at the small-time airport and the cold dampness that enveloped it, situated anywhere else it could only have been thought of as dreary.

"Welcome to the Gros Morne Mountains, Once Part of the Great Appalachian Range!" a tourist sign boasted as she drove up towards St. Carol's. But the magnitude of these mountains had diminished for Ann since she'd left home; they appeared to be receding inland. The hills arced down gently towards the sea, into meadows and wetlands peppered with wildflowers. There were splotches of red and orange now, which reminded her of a wool cap she had worn for years as a child. September was the month he had always gone hunting.

"You might get to see some bergs, they says dere's an ice island the size of Manhattan coming down the coast, never heard of this time of year," said the receptionist at the unimaginatively named Rocky's hotel in Rocky Harbour. "Thanks," was all Ann said, sensing the woman was nosy (something tourists labelled as friendly). She did not want to share the reason they were heading up the coast, or how it added to her heartbreak to be reminded that Greenland was melting, or her general feeling little could be salvaged on a single trip home.

"I'm eating a feed of Chips, D and G," Doris said to Ann on the phone when she called.

"Aren't you supposed to watch what you eat, didn't the doctor tell you stay away from fried foods?" Ann said.

"Well, Judy and the girls wanted to treat me."

"What about your diabetes?"

"I only got a few things left I enjoys. Can't wait to see you."

"OK, well, take it easy, eh."

"I do miss 'im now that he's gone. Oh, Sunday Uncle Joe will take us out to the Grey Islands, that's where he wanted to be laid to rest. Out where the ocean can carry him away."

Ann took an Ativan and lay on the sagging bed, covered with a worn homemade quilt.

In the bathroom, half-drugged, she stood and looked in the mirror. In foreign mirrors you saw yourself in a state of flux, an actor who played the role of you in a smaller episode of your larger life. Only in your home mirror did you really see yourself.

Once Ann heard a story on the CBC about a performance artist who didn't look in a mirror for a year. Unable to see herself the artist became more attentive of other faces, their strange and innumerable varieties.

Ann looked at her skin: the flaccidity of it, the fluidity and soft excess of her body.

"Did ye get yer skin last night?" the b'ys in St. Anthony used to say the day after a high school dance.

More like her father than she would have wanted to admit, she liked to wander alone along the river and marvel at the variety of foliage, or even stroll in steely downtown after work, in the glass canyon; she found joy in abundance, a relief from interviewing strangers on the phone who came and went so quickly in and out of her life that they made her feel lonely. She could lose herself for hours in the supermarket. Doris showed her love through food until the two were partially intertwined in Ann's mind. She had her mother's "big boned" frame, those were her father's words; Rubenesque, her mother called her.

When Ann had left for the tar sands when the boom began, to work in classifieds for a small paper and live with her aunt near Fort Mac, her old man had said:

"So, we'll see you soon."

"It won't be for awhile, Dad."

"Yes, I s'pose. Just be careful, and do what your aunt says. People will take yer money. Some expensive there, so dey says."

"Clary, she's not in with the crowd you knows, b'y, she's not going wasting her money on bars and foolishness — there's lots of work and other things to do," her mother said.

"For now. But that'll be gone. Sure the fishery's gone, the country's gone, the whole world is gone," he'd said.

And now he was gone, too.

When she stepped outside to take in the air of Rocky Harbour, Ann knew that she had changed, knew she had flown away and planted her seeds somewhere else. However this trip turned out, she was not her mother.

But she also knew that only when she got back to Calgary would she be able to truly see this trip's meaning, like a climber who goes back to base camp to evaluate progress, to measure their adaptability to the change in altitude. Only when she was back in her new home, only then, would she know what she had lost.

•••

PAUL WHITTLE *was born and raised in St. John's. He began writing while completing a degree in English literature in 1999. Since then he has won Newfoundland and Labrador Arts and Letters' awards for poetry and prose. His writing has been published in Tickleace, The Newfoundland Quarterly, and in "The Backyards of Heaven." In 2012 he had a residency at the Banff Arts Centre to work on a collection of short stories. One story in the collection, "Everything is What it is," was shortlisted for the 2009 CBC literary awards. He holds a master's degree in English literature at Memorial University, where he works in marketing and communications.*

Smoke Rings

By Frank Barry

I can't go on.

Outside my window, the cold fog and freezing drizzle have sunk their icicle fangs deep into the slushy flesh of another interminable Newfoundland spring. I am becoming catatonic. Only the intermittent twitching of my left eyeball, surely a symptom of severe nicotine deprivation, informs me that I have not yet crossed over into the vale. The sun has not been seen in months. Its existence is now officially a myth.

Look at it out there. Gloomy as a mole's rectum.

The cheque should come today but not for sure, nothing in this world is for sure. I know that now. Except tobacco.

How long can a person go on dying for a cigarette without actually dying? I blow a circle of breath on the windowpane and draw the vague memory of a smoke-ring. Gazing through it my heart suddenly leaps with reckless hope at what might be the faintest glimpse of a feeble ray of sun. But no, the tiny yellow smudge, signifying light and life, is drawn quietly back behind the cold wet blanket of fog and silently dispatched. Was it even there?

Wild fantasies assail my nicotine-deprived brain.

Me jumping over the counter at Needs.

Me kicking buddy in the knobs.

Me grabbing a pack of Matinee Extra Lights, flaring one up and inhaling it straight down to its golden filter tip in one long orgasmic suck, moments before the encircling SWAT team's expert marksman explodes my inflamed brain with a high-powered bullet.

If only.

If only someone I know would walk up the street so that I could bum a smoke. If only some bum would walk up the street so that I could bum a smoke. Bum a smoke bum a smoke bum a smoke. I've already sold my empties.

Why didn't I finish university? I'd have smokes now. Cartons of them.

Where in the fog is the mailman? At the same time … if the mailman comes … but the cheque. … I can't let myself contemplate that. The razor is too keen. Too close at hand.

Where, dear God, is the sun? Where, dear God, is the cigarette?

The glowing end of a cigarette can be one's own little sun. With a cigarette between my lips my life would be different. I'd be like some heroic French resistance-fighter who roams the misty streets, thinking hard and sucking deeply, while secretly distributing his clandestine pamphlets inciting the petite bourgeoisie to take up arms against their cruel conquerors. I'd teach those fascist bastards to ban smoking in bars!

But without a smoke? What can one do without a smoke? The question answers itself.

The French always seem to have cigarettes. Like in the movies. Pierre, Robert and Guillaume shackled together in some Nazi torture dungeon but still passing round the smokes. I can hear them now.

Pierre: "This is zee end. Tomorrow we face deeth. "

Robert: "In zee end, everyone must face deeth."

Guillaume: "True. Zee end is near — but time enough is there to light up and enjoy fully this flavour-packed carton of Gitane before we must face deeth. Vive Tabac!"

Where did they get them? Did the Nazis open a little kiosk so the French torturees wouldn't have to suffer nicotine withdrawal?

Oberstleutnant Schmidt: "The rack? Ya! Ya! But make zem do without zee zigarette? Vee are not munsters! Heil Filter!"

Life isn't fair. Right now I'd dance to the rack for a pack of smokes.

Wait — did I check down behind the cushions? I know I did. Why do I always give myself up to false hope?

Is that the mailman? No it's a pigeon. Pigeons don't smoke. French pigeons probably smoke. Ceaselessly.

He flew away.

God I'm lonely.

The new girl behind the counter? She's cute. I think she likes me. Not enough to sneak me a free pack of smokes though. You'd probably have to be married to someone for a hundred years before they'd commit to that degree of larceny. But she does like me. I'd marry her grandmother for a pack of smokes. Better make it a case. Grandmothers live a long time nowadays.

I could sell some books down at Afterwords. I'd only get about 10 cents each for them. I'd have to sell 80 books to get a pack of smokes. Do I even have 80 books? Stupid books are what got me here in the first place.

Oh, the pigeon came back. Looks like the same one. Yup there he goes — peck-peck-pecking. Read enough books and the next thing you know you think you can write one. I'd be better off trying to smoke one.

I don't think that is the same pigeon. This one seems to have a stronger work ethic.

Wow — 80 books equal a pack of smokes. Take that, Tolstoy. He smoked. Like a Labrador tilt. Or was that Gorky? One of them. One of them always had smokes. Not like me.

What's that moving in the window across the street? The neighbour's cat. God I hate cats. They really think they're something.

Do I exist merely to crave a cigarette? I crave, therefore I am? Please shut up.

Maybe I should write about this experience. This non-experience.

Has anything ever been written without a cigarette?

I'd need a title. Hmmm … got it! "An Essay On The Non-Experience Experienced While Not Smoking A Nonexistent Cigarette." That pretty well sums it up. My most self-cannibalizing title yet. A perfect ouroboros of meaninglessness devouring nothingness. Why bother to write the essay? To add anything further would be an insult to the reader. Oh yes — we mustn't forget "dear" reader. Hauled off in his wing-backed chair before the fireplace, wrapped in his silken smoking-jacket, swirling a brandy and stoking his full-bodied, eight-inch hand-rolled Presidente whilst blowing his sky-blue and ever widening smoke rings forever heavenwards. No we mustn't forget that self-satisfied bastard.

Dear God, now I'm cursing the nonexistent reader of my nonexistent essay about a nonexistent cigarette.

I've read stories about seamen on far voyages that were reduced to smoking rope. Wouldn't it have been easier to make a noose? I don't have any rope. I'm completely ropeless.

Writing? Har har har. Don't get me started. It's on the wall my friend. And it isn't your universally rejected and gleefully excoriated experimental children's book — "The Dog Hanging." Unbelievably gratuitous violence, they said. Try autobiographically gratuitous violence, I thought.

Nonexistent is a funny word.

Who's that?

It's the mailman! It is! Oh, you sweet handsomely paid for walking around without a care in the world uniform-wearing man — I love you.

Wait — what's he doing? You filthy cur! I hate you! Come back!

Just … passed … on … by.

In his stupid uniform.

Stormtrooper.

I wonder if he has any smokes. Should I chase after him? He's gone. Why don't you take my broken ashtray of a heart with you, you bastard?

It isn't his fault. Got a family to feed. A smoke-free family, probably. Bastards.

I can't go on.

What will happen now?

Is this how I must end?

I wonder if the cushions on the chesterfield are stuffed with horse-hair.

Is it the same pigeon?

•••

FRANK BARRY *was born and raised in St. John's. In 1979 he co-founded the Sheila's Brush Theatre Co. for which he wrote many theatre works. He is the author and co-author of over 30 dramatic works, several of which have been published by nationally based publishers. He has twice been awarded the Newfoundland and Labrador Arts and Letters Awards, once for drama and once for poetry. He is currently writing for stage and film, with his short film "The Days of Mary" in post-production.*

The Countdown

By Mike Daly

George had excellent eyesight. Without it, it would have been impossible to discern the movements of the fly's legs, and he needed to count its steps. He deduced that the fly used three legs in concert: outside two on the right, inside one on the left, followed by the opposite. He counted seven steps before the insect took flight and disappeared into the unseen recesses of the dirty, gloomy bar. Satisfied, he exhaled and sipped his soda.

George requested fruit in his soda so it would appear more exotic and alcoholic. Sitting alone in a bar was one thing, but sitting alone without booze was something else entirely. He craved his solitude, yet loved public places. Alcohol no longer brought him either pleasure or escape, so he drank his soda, hoping no one would notice him.

An air of easiness hung about as people floated from one group to the next, with strangers striking allegiances of circumstance. George knew nothing of the emotional ebb and flow that surrounded each exchange. His hand reached into his long sleeve, tugged free the razor blade sewn there, and cut a fresh line into his middle forearm. The scar-to-be melded amongst the countless others. A red handkerchief was stowed and sewed surreptitiously up his sleeve to capture the blood.

George neither heard nor saw the approach of the filthy little man who sat down, announcing himself with a forceful slap against the table top, shocking George into sucking in a stray cube of ice and getting it lodged in his throat. The cube hung there, slowly melting itself out of existence. The suffocating feeling was rather quite delightful. It passed momentarily.

"Whoo-wee! Sorry, Jimmy," said the filthy man, "thought I'd gotten you good there for a second."

The man wore a cloud of dust and desperation over dirty clothes, looking as if he had come a long way down a hard road. He slumped down in the chair opposite George, appearing to melt into the wood.

"My name is not Jimmy."

The man eyed him hazily. "You sure about that?"

"Quite."

"Suit yourself. All the same, any chance you could by an old pal a drink, Jimmy?"

George stared at him. Filthy Man met his gaze in flickers and jolts, looking rather feral. George raised his hand, caught the bartender's eye, and pointed down towards Filthy Man's beer. The bartender sauntered over with a dewy bottle. George paid wordlessly and watched the bartender stride away. Eight steps to get to the table, five steps to return.

Filthy Man talked and George listened until he drifted away into his own thoughts. He spoke of lost days, friends and loves, but only snippets snuck into George's ear. George tried counting how often he blinked, but his eyes were so bloodshot and thin that it was infuriatingly difficult to discern when the real blinks occurred. While he talked, George's hand managed to slip in two fresh slices with his razor.

Filthy Man blinked once. "You're good listener, you know that?"

George stared.

"You wanna know a secret?" He blinked twice. "I've got a priceless work of art."

"Indeed."

Filthy Man leaned close, his voice dropping to a whisper.

"It's true. You wanna see it?"

George looked once more to see if the fly had returned. It hadn't. Filthy Man's blinks were now suspiciously absent.

"Yes," said George.

They left the bar, stepping into the cool breezes of Water Street. The walk was short. One-hundred-and-sixty-four paces for Filthy Man, 126 for George.

George contemplated the mechanics of the man's gait. Did a stumble or a stagger count as a step? If so, how many steps would it take sober? Filthy Man continued speaking while George's mind struggled with conjecture. Smugglers ... thieves ... run aground ... St. Pierre ... my darling ... anonymity ... Newfoundland.

"You're in for a treat. Truly, a treat."

They soon stood before Filthy Man's house. It was squat and slanted, and pressed tightly to the road. George felt it looked like a playhouse, and behind the doors he expected to find dolls and toys and Easy-Bake Ovens baking imaginary pies.

"Come in, Jimmy, come in."

George crouched low to avoid the top of the tiny doorframe and hunkered inside. To the right, a tiny stairway led to a tiny upstairs, and to the left, tiny doorways led to tiny rooms. Filthy Man stumbled straight ahead to his little play-kitchen.

"Tea, Jimmy! Tea with rum for us!"

George's hand sliced a fresh notch into his arm. He thought it might be time to give the left a break and move on to the right.

The house had snippets of newspapers and decaying pieces of art smeared on the clapboard walls. Stains that looked and smelled of vomit and blood littered the floors. George walked to the stairs and peered up into the darkness. He wondered what happened in those recesses. He returned to the kitchen and found Filthy Man at the table, dead asleep.

George watched him move and mutter incoherently like a dog dreaming of rabbits. Sweat sprouted on Filthy Man's brow, and his eyelids fluttered from his imaginings. He watched Filthy Man's chest rise and fall sporadically, and his lips move curses and poetry in his sleep. George fingered his razor blade, stepped forward and reached for him, but then saw the pulsing, regular rhythm of his jugular. Entranced, George sighed, looked up, and saw her.

She was the only framed thing in the house. She peered out ominously, taking ownership of the room. Her red hair cascaded, and her skin was supple and pristine. He played his eyes over her, pushing away the background that seemed to jump and swim behind her. He looked to her mouth, curved like a scimitar, tasting the words that wanted to come from her lips. Her nose, sweet and simple. Her eyes. Oh my. His breath, sharply taken, then lost. Her eyes held him, pushing and pulling, following his every shift and shuffle. He reached up and touched her, fingers delicately tracing the rises and falls of the brushstrokes. He played his fingers over her mouth, tracing her jaw up beyond her cheeks, and finally sweeping across her eyes, so beautiful and wise. What, he wondered, what are you thinking? What do you want of me? Please stop looking at me like that. Please … don't stop.

A dull clang of metal on arborite rousted him. He looked to the table and saw his razor blade, stained with blood, resting there. It must have slipped from his grip. He looked from it to Filthy Man, then back to her. She was so out of place in this house of guilt and neglect. He wanted to take her, but it didn't matter. She was in him, and somehow she chose also to be there.

He left and emerged into the cool St. John's evening. He tasted the salt air. A young couple walked by, holding hands and laughing. He wondered what was funny, and knowing he might never understand, he smiled. Feeling the chill he decided for home, counting his steps, but by the time he got there, he had completely lost track.

•••

MIKE DALY *is a writer, actor, and filmmaker from St. John's. He has travelled and worked and lived abroad, but has been drawn back to Newfoundland, his home. This is his first Cuffer Prize entry, written with inspiration found from this place and some great creative friends who share his love of writing.*

The Dumpers

By Robin Reid

There is a trail off the old Highway 56 which will take you past a sparkling jade-blue lake in Central. You may hear the caw-cawing of a family of crows which have taken up residence in the evergreen trees crowding the lakeshores.

In the far distance across the lake, you may glimpse the odd old shack of a cabin, but there are few to be seen. Sometimes you may see someone in a dory slinging a fishing line across the still waters.

Rarely is there a power boat to disturb the tranquility of the lake. I have fished often in these waters and I can vouch for the plentiful trout available to the patient fisher, human or avian. I work in the city but I waste no time in getting out to this rural area for relaxation and recovery. My work is stressful and my doctor has suggested that I slow down, take it easy. He fears the onset of my Alzheimer's is getting more severe. He is even considering suspending my driving privileges. Until that time, I intend to get out to my cabin by the lake as often as I can.

It was while on one of my strolls along the lakeshore that I thought I saw something metallic gleaming deep in the woods. This disturbed me. It should not be there! I took my hunting rifle — my grandfather's old 306 — and headed off the trail towards the metal-sheen. Rabbits bounded away from me into the woods as I stealthily made my way forward. I knelt behind some bushes and spotted "them," the Dumpers.

There were two of them. One, in a yellow shirt, was dragging an old fridge off their pickup truck, which was a Ford F-150. The other one, in a red shirt, was directing him while standing on a large battered metal container. Other debris were scattered about the clearing making an awful mess.

Already the crows were picking at it, tearing open orange garbage bags and strewing pieces around. I was taken aback by this desecration of my pastoral patrol by the lake. I could not even remember in the chaos of my mind whether or not I had loaded my 306 that morning before setting out.

No matter. These Dumpers would not know if my rifle was loaded. It looked menacing enough, I'm sure.

I stepped out of the brush and leveled the rifle in their direction. I thought they would bolt into the woods but instead they stared at me, slack-jawed, and raised their hands.

Immediately, they started pleading their case. The stuff was not really their garbage; they were just doing a friend a favour. They knew it was wrong and apologized. They would pick it all up and be on their way and sorry for the trouble, skipper.

I may be old and have Alzheimer's or dementia or whatever you call it, but I'm not stupid. As soon as I was gone, they'd be back and dump garbage all over the woods, if not here then nearby.

I snarled at them to start picking up all the rubbish which the crows had strewn about. This they did at speed and placed it all back in the F-150. Only the metal container and fridge were left derelict in the bushes.

They protested at first when I made them hand over their cellphones. Yet they did so quickly when I brought the 306 up to my eye to fire. They both filled the air with expletives about a "crazy old coot," but I got their cellphones all right.

Next, I motioned to the one in the red shirt to get into the metal box. I told yellow shirt to open the fridge and see if he would fit right in there. Suddenly, they both started babbling at once saying they were only young fellers about to head out to Alberta to look for work.

This did not move me at all. I was determined to make an example of these two who so casually tried to destroy my woods by dumping their junk by my lake.

Red shirt went into the metal container quite handily. I snapped the lock in place as I listened to his pathetic whimpers. There were rust holes in the sides so he would not suffocate.

At gunpoint, yellow shirt disappeared inside the fridge. He was the smaller of these two vandals yet even so the fit was quite snug. The door closed securely and, as with red shirt's container, there were rust holes to prevent suffocation.

The F-150's keys were in the ignition so I started up the truck and drove out of the clearing onto the trail. I could already hear thumping coming from the container and fridge as I drove off. In the morning, I shall return and let red shirt and yellow shirt out.

I drove down Highway 56 a few kilometres and had a coffee and Jiggs dinner at the Dildo Diner.

I left the F-150 with the cellphones on the seat in the parking lot. I took a cab back to my cabin by the lake.

I told the cabbie I got lost while hunting. The rifle was never even loaded after all.

It has been four days since I met red shirt and yellow shirt. I meant to release them the next day but I could not find the way. It is strange because I have walked in these woods and along the lake so many times.

I have heard a helicopter skimming through the sky looking for the Dumpers. On the news it was reported that their F-150 truck was found at the parking lot of Dildo Diner. Their cellphones were left on the seat in the truck.

I will continue to look for them and I'm sure I will find them eventually. I was going to search again today but I saw a blue pickup loaded with garbage bags and an old washing machine drive down a dirt road by the other shore of the lake. I better take care of the blue pickup first. I won't forget to load my 306 this time.

One thing on the news puzzled me: it was reported that the two most recent missing men were the latest of several disappearances of people around the lakeshore area.

I better be careful.

•••

ROBIN REID is a long-term resident of St. John's. He has travelled to most areas of Canada. He has a lively interest in many subjects, especially legal matters and military history.

The End of the World

By Jacqueline Clarke

Mags sank her shovel into the soft flesh of the earth. This was her favourite chore. She hated churning butter, she hated checking the catch for signs of disease and she hated fixing the ridiculous fence that surrounded her family's meagre property. But this, the digging, the planting, the tending, that was her favourite chore. She loved her family's garden.

They never had the money for livestock, and with her father on the boats most of the time, and her mother constantly ill with her headaches, money was scarce. Whatever Mags could grow in their garden was the money that put food on the table. She wasn't much of a house-woman; making bread and cooking meals never really agreed with her. Her little sister was better at that. Mags had a knack for this, finding untainted soil that could still produce crops, best crops in the town of Johns.

The routine calmed her, cleared her brain. She didn't have to think about the fact that most of her father's catch would come home with the disease, passed down for generations since the Last Great War, when the world blew itself up and killed each other off. Since, only small places like the island of New Found Land remained, but they were harmed all the same. No one was unaffected. Deformities were the norm, and healthy humans, such as her, were automatically set for marriage, in hopes of creating children that didn't hold the disease.

Mags herself was to be married in the morning to a boy that lived in the centre, a wealthier area of Johns. It was an unusual pairing, usually they try to keep it within their wealth districts, but for their group, the numbers of healthies were lower. They made do with what they had.

Mags continued to dig. Her gut clenched at the thought of Barrett, her paired groom. Because with the thought of Barrett came the thought of Anchor, and with the thought of Anchor, she dug harder.

And as usual, he read her thoughts.

"Hey Scruff, keep digging and you'll land yourself in hell," laughed a deep, resonating voice. Anchor was leaning on her shaky fence. A sharp wind blew through the alley where he stood, ruffling his longish, light brown hair. He didn't shiver, despite his thin shirt. He stood tall. Poor, through and through, he had the pride of the poor.

He was a few years Mags' senior, and their fathers shared duty on the same fishing boat. The oldest of five young ones, Anchor spent his time doing whatever he could to provide. The only problem with him was his lame leg. It looked normal enough, but it never worked properly. He was one of the diseased. He couldn't get any jobs outside of handiwork around the town. So he made sure he did a damn fine job of doing it.

Mags straightened up and stared at Anchor. He was one of the best-looking men in town, girls took note of it, and he had a line of diseased women waiting for their chance. Strong jaw, fit body, it was hard to believe he was born with the disease. Just that damned leg.

"Shag off, Anchor. I need to make sure this is done before tomorrow," she carelessly shot back. Tomorrow. There it was again. She would be moved into the house Barrett's parents have bought and fixed up for them. She wondered had Anchor worked on it. Her gut threatened to heave.

A look flickered across Anchor's usually stony face, but Mags couldn't decipher it.

"The young ones will be fine, Mags," Anchor said softly, meeting her eyes. "Lola isn't as useless as you think she is. She can bake. She has watched you tend that garden for years. And Cougar will figure it out. He's a smart lad." With the thought of not being around to tend to Lola and Cougar while her mother died from the disease, Mags fell to her knees in the muck, dirtying her freshly mended pants.

"Oh little Scruff," whispered Anchor. With that he limped around the fence to her yard, settling himself on the cold ground next to her, lame leg splayed straight in front of him. He put one strong arm around her, drawing her close. "They'll be fine. I'll make sure of it. Lola hasn't got any sign of the disease either, your family is lucky. She will be married off too. Cougar is only deaf in one ear. He is able-bodied. He'll be fine. Worry about you."

Mags rested her head on his shoulder. If the Council got wind of this, Anchor handling a paired wife, he'd suffer the stocks and some jail time. Her eyes looked above at the grey sky, the weak sun trying to cut through. She wished she had control over the weather. Or anything, for that matter. She wished she had pretended to be deaf in one ear, to not have registered healthy. The doctors would have figured it out, but who knows. The poor were often overlooked anyway.

"I don't want to marry him Anchor. I don't want to marry him at all," she whispered. "I don't want to bear any kind of child for him." She felt Anchor stiffen underneath her head.

"These pairings be damned. The disease is in all of us. Haven't they learned the damage is so far done that it doesn't matter who pairs with whom? The doctors should know it by now. I don't even think it's about that anymore. It's control, Mags, control from the Council."

"If that was true, why the hell would a poor like me be paired with a wealth like Barrett?" Mags asked, perturbed. Anchor barked a laugh.

"Oh little Scruff. Have you ever looked at yourself? You're so beautiful. Blond hair like gold, green eyes like the grass during a good summer, body that is fit and sound. When you laugh, it lights up the entire market and when you smile, everyone wishes it was for them. Barrett wanted a beautiful wife, and a healthy wife."

Mags snorted. "The pool of contenders was small." And with that, Anchor gently turned her head and kissed her softly. She froze. It was undemanding, it was slow. His lips were soft, but persistent. After a hesitation, she melted into his arms, responding with the years of pent-up anticipation of secretly wondering what it would be like to kiss Anchor. And as softly and suddenly as it started, it ended. She studied his jaw as he turned away from her and stared at the fence, away from Mags. Her gut clenched again.

"My pool was always just one," he whispered huskily, staring at the fence.

Mags grasped his hand tightly, letting him be her Anchor.

•••

JACQUELINE CLARKE *is from the Burin Peninsula and currently lives and works in St. John's. She is a young adult novel enthusiast and a sucker for a good love story. She writes as much as she can in her spare time.*

Come Home Year

By Nathan Downey

So there we were, my brothers and I, ankles mired in the bog, the perfume of alder leaves and slower smells — decay, the ponderous grip of seasons — hanging on the August air. The Codroy River was a skein of silver far below us as the sun plummeted into the western hills.

"Christ, how is there a bog up here? I thought we were climbing a hill," Jason said.

I couldn't stop myself from replying about topography, the slope of the hill, gravity. As a coping mechanism, I become an insufferable pedant in situations of uncertainty.

And sure enough, Adam snapped at me. "Oh my God, shut up, Steven! Whose idea was it to do this?"

A second cousin had driven us up. Joe Sams. We had never met this man before, or maybe we did during one of our family trips to Newfoundland, on one of those days where we'd visit five or six houses full of relatives in a single day, perching in their living rooms, smelling molasses buns or boiled vegetables, eyeing the decorative barometer-thermometer combination on the wall, resisting on pain of grounding the impulse to squirm and pick at each other while our parents caught up with Aunt Martha or Aunt Elsie or whoever. Joe wasn't at our father's funeral that I can recall but he certainly knew who he was.

"Francis, oh yes. Sad to see him go, though he was off to Alberta all them years ago anyway," he said. Joe had our same last name. Everyone in Codroy, it seemed, had our last name.

He had driven us up a gravel road that traversed the valley's southern flank. Like kids, Jason and I rode in the bed. We had been sharing a pack of cigarettes since the funeral, though neither of us had smoked for years. Adam, always the older brother, rode disapprovingly in the cab with Cousin Joe. Joe drove us to the uppermost limit of the road, telling us to follow the track through the alders up over the brow of the hill and we'd eventually reach the pond. The Pond.

We marched up the heavily overgrown trail, grass and bracken pulling at our ankles. At some point, we must have lost our bearings altogether because the alders fell away and we ended up in the bog.

Jason and Adam were carrying packs full of camping gear. In my backpack I had a sleeping bag and my father, what was left of him, in a two-litre container that had once held orange-pineapple ice cream.

"Could the man have picked a more inconvenient place?" I asked, exasperated.

The truth of it was his death had been inconvenient, too. A heart attack at 75, while golfing. Only they were in South Africa, stop 14 on my mother's retirement campaign to see the world. It was sad and sudden. No one tells you, though, about the logistical hassles a family member's death entails, the nagging administrivia that taint the acrid sapidity of grief with notes of frustration and impatience.

I had flown to Durban to meet my mother. Getting there took four flights and two Valium. We cremated him there, filling out a raft of paperwork to take the ashes out of Africa. I half jokingly suggested strewing him on the savannah to blow around like topsoil. To become part of watering holes and mud wallows. But my mother insisted that he would want to be scattered in Newfoundland. And so we held the funeral there, in Corner Brook. Jason came from Victoria, where he worked as a music teacher. Both of us had to strong-arm Adam, whom neither of us had seen in years, into coming at all. But in the end we were all there.

His funeral was more of a party than any I'd been to. It was the first I'd attended in Newfoundland. Everyone got monumentally drunk on Old Sams and moonshine relatives from Codroy had brought. There was even a band and I swear to God it just materialized unbidden and wasn't out of place in the least.

When his will was read, there was one baffling codicil lurking among his open-handed bequests.

I wish to be cremated; my ashes are to be scattered at The Pond in Codroy Valley.

Decoding this niggling, vague dying wish meant pumping his grieving sisters for information. Aunts Melinda and Liz decided he was referring to a spot in the hills where he'd gone trouting with his father in the summers of his youth. This information had led to a bigger question: how were we supposed to find the damned place?

Perhaps incited by our liquor-addled keening, my brothers and I decided to scatter the ashes together and it seemed feasible enough despite our total unfamiliarity with the western island. How hard could it really be, if he'd gone there as a kid? We traveled to Codroy Valley a few days after the will was read and stayed with my father's cousin, Walter. On the drive in, I experienced one of the fleeting moments in my life when a geographical feature reconciled with the archetype in my head. Over cards and rum we had discussed our strategy and arranged for a ride up the rugged gravel road.

Cursing heavily, flybitten and sweating, we now pulled our way through the bog, one sodden footfall at a time, crossing the expanse to where an uplift of land stood on the far end, crowned with more alders. Free at last from the quagmire, we charged up through the thicket of trees.

Our shoes squished audibly as we groped our way through the woods. Heaving, panting, we broke our way through branches and snarls for another 10 minutes or so. And there it stood, finally, gleaming in the day's last sunlight, its surface a mirror of the fading sky, broken at intervals by breaching trout. The air throbbed with the song of insects.

We stood on the shore, each holding a handful of ashes.

"Good fishing, Pops," I eulogized, and the words sounded flat in the sticky air. We stood awkwardly for a moment, and then threw the ashes into the pond in ragged unison, some of the bigger bits entering with a splash, some settling onto the surface in wisps, like mayflies.

After, we drank a bottle of whisky, passing it between us and saying little. A menacing stack of clouds mounted above the pond, flowing in from the west. Suddenly the sweltering air broke around us and the wind started ripping through the alders, torturing the burnished surface of the pond. We were driven into the tent as fat raindrops came pummeling down. The crash of thunder caromed off the sides of the valley. We lay on our sleeping bags, soaked, and the tent's walls heaved like sailcloth.

"I thought thunderstorms didn't happen in Newfoundland. I thought it was all drizzle and fog," Adam said.

"Jesus, we're gonna die in this. The tent poles are made of carbon fibre," I groaned. We lay on our backs, watching the sky, huge and coruscant, roiling above us through the thin nylon of the tent. And all three of us started to laugh.

•••

NATHAN DOWNEY *is a writer and editor living in St. John's. He is a graduate of Memorial University and a native of Alberta.*

Mercy

By Grant Loveys

This is the way it always goes. The same dream most nights and the rest as empty as the other side of the bed: us taking tea on Nipper Hill, that giant wedge in the blueberry bog God drove and we conquered back when we weren't too busy trying to conquer each other. A few stars left in the sky like the grit I heard in your voice when you said, "Look for me in the next life" — the same grit still pluming in my heart. Table set, tea poured, and two of us together again; just twin piles of bones to cross the skull moon we sit beneath. And it's been so long since everything ended these dreams hold you only as a vague suggestion, some approximation like a smoke cloud through lace.

That's the problem with memory — you lose what you want to keep and lose control over what you want to forget. It's like buckshot coming up through flesh. One day there's just an itch and a dark spot beneath the skin, and the next morning there's a clink on the bathroom floor and the warmth of your palm on my chest again.

At the table I ask for one last night together, but you're willing the sun up after half a cup, antsy as ever, ready for the climb. I'd always thought I was the impatient one, but I was only ever impatient with you. So much of you to see, to discover; how it felt to catch your cold, the certain way you slurped spaghetti, the secret sounds you made only for me. But I could always hear the clock ticking.

When the sun finally cracks the bay you're up from your chair and stomping up the hill, 10 feet ahead in a second, the sight of your back no easier now than ever. I'm trying to think of one perfect sentence, some combination of syllables that would turn you around, bring you back to the table, bring you back to me. I never do. I just chase you through endless blueberry bog that purples our bare feet, moving ever closer to the top and what comes next. I say so many things — bits of old conversation, clipped snatches of words we shared, my memory kept close — but not one I love you or I miss you or I need you. No help from my throat. Just waves of dream babble breaking on the shores of your back. When we reach the top, you walk right to the cliff's edge and curl your toes around the crumbling stone. In the bay below, the monolithic shadow of a whale moving through the depths, immense and secreted and entirely alive, like the things we thought but never said.

Then another memory comes up through the skin — the time we went fishing in Salmonier. The time you reeled in a thick trout and left it to die alone and gasping on a rock. I thought you cruel for doing so and said as much, and I guess that was the moment everything began to end. But tonight, with you wavering on the cliff's edge, I remember it differently. Maybe you didn't have it in you to end something perfect so savagely. Maybe you left it to find its own way to the end because you didn't know how to deal with so much unspoken suffering.

This is what will remain in the morning — my assumptions of your motives, all my error. My cold company as I sit on the edge of the bed, filled as completely with memory's buckshot as the pearled roe that swelled the belly of our lost and dying trout.

But for now you turn your head, baring only the ripe suggestion of your cheek. Another few degrees and I'd have your eyes again, or the nose I kissed so many times — some piece of wreckage I can cling to. "Does it have to be this way?" I whisper, but you don't answer. You never do. Eventually I turn away, my question caught on the sea breeze, and begin back down. A few seconds later the bay swallows wetly, sending gulls blooming across the sun entwined in each other.

Nipper Hill still stands, rising over Conception Bay as it always has, looking just as it did on the day we stumbled blinking from our own separate paths only to meet in the middle and hike a shared one to the top. Does it remember cradling us as we lay together in the sunshine and I painted my name on your belly with blueberry guts? Does it have some armour against the neutering stillness of forever, to ward off the earth's restless esthetic? Does anything? All of us — hill, trout, you and I — will eventually depart to our own particular kinds of nothing. Maybe you'll come back to me before then with an armload of answers. I hope so. But as one more day dawns red behind my eyelids, I am just trying to remember how to forget you.

•••

GRANT LOVEYS *is the author of "Our Gleaming Bones Unrobed" (ECW Press, 2012), and has won several awards for his work, including a 2010 Arts and Letters Award for poetry and the 2011 Cuffer Prize. He lives in St. John's.*

Snares

By Michael Finn

It turned out to be just a rabbit.

Francis had been startled by a rustling in the alders bordering the trail. He'd stopped, his heart pounding, afraid it might be a bear or coyote. With muscles tensed and breath held, he'd stifled the fear rippling up his spine. Perhaps he shouldn't have rushed ahead. But nothing had growled or pounced on him, so he'd pushed aside the branches and peered into the undergrowth.

The rabbit was huddled against the ground, its neck connected by a taut silver thread to a branch above its run. But it had not drawn the wire tight enough. Now it crouched on the dried leaves, a bundle of beige fur frozen in stillness.

He wondered what thoughts were flitting through its rabbit brain, what it was feeling, whether it was afraid of him.

His father was not far behind. He would know what to do, how to free the rabbit. If he tried it himself he might hurt it even more. He could see that the snare had bitten deep into its fur.

He crept nearer and knelt to inspect it. As he edged closer, the rabbit twitched and lurched for a couple of seconds before freezing again. Careful, careful, he thought. Couldn't small creatures die of fright? He inched back a foot or so, feeling the damp leaves through the knees of his jeans.

Pools of jet glistened in its moist brown eyes, which stared straight ahead. Maybe the rabbit was thinking that it could make him go away by concentrating on some distant object in the undergrowth. Its flattened ears and even its whiskers were still. But when he leaned to look closer he noticed a subtle shivering, as if the rabbit were struggling to subdue a force its body could barely restrain.

"Hey," he said. "Take it easy. My dad'll set you free."

He crept backwards, stood up and retreated to the trail to see how far behind his father was. He listened carefully to distinguish the tread of his father's boots from the sound of the wind in the treetops and the muted turbulence of the river.

While Francis waited he studied his surroundings. His father was always telling him to be observant, to pay attention to things, to notice details.

But there was little chance of getting lost this close to the Exploits. Through the gaps between the trees he saw the tall reddish-brown smokestack of the defunct paper mill. Further back at the beginning of the trail was the bridge spanning the gorge where the river flowed behind the mill. Walking across it with his father, he'd paused to gaze between its girders at the churning whitewater far below. Even this far up the trail he could still hear the river, its rumble diminished to a distant angry whisper.

He was about to creep back into the bushes to check on the rabbit when he heard his father calling. Not wanting to frighten it even more by shouting a reply, Francis headed back to meet him.

When Jackman saw his son approaching he knew right away the boy was excited about something. Francis was breathless, his cheeks flushed.

His son's pleasure in his father's company helped allay the strain of the three-weeks-on, one-week-off turnaround of Jackman's new Alberta job. After 18 steady years in the mill it was hard to have to leave home for work. He wasn't resentful, though. Anyone with a clue could have seen the shutdown coming. And as the crowd at Tim's was always saying, you had to do what you had to do. Still, though. It was hard. Hard on his wife, hard on him, hard on Francis. But he had to hand it to the boy. At 10 he was becoming resilient and self-sufficient. The way he forged ahead during their hikes revealed an independence and confidence that helped ease Jackman's misgivings about having to be away for so long.

"Dad," Francis said. "Guess what?"

"You tell me."

"Up ahead."

"Yeah? What's up ahead?"

"Up ahead, there's a rabbit in a snare."

"Oh yeah?"

"And he's alive."

Jackman's pace slowed. He looked at the boy, saw both eagerness and concern in his blue eyes.

"Still alive, is he? How do you know?"

Francis could barely restrain an urge to run back to where he'd heard the rabbit scrabbling in the leaves.

"Quick," he said. "Come on, Dad. I'll show you."

Then his son was gone again, and when he caught up a minute later he saw the boy kneeling at the edge of a clump of alders.

"Come here, Dad. Look, just look." The hush of his voice could not suppress an undercurrent of urgency, of fear.

Jackman bent to peer over Francis's shoulder. Sure enough, the boy was right. He also saw how deep the wire had bitten, and knew that freeing the animal would make no difference. The right thing to do would be to kill it. He knew that he would do this, and he knew it would be a long time before his son understood or forgave him.

"Francis," he said.

"Can't you free him, Dad? Hey?"

"Francis, look at him."

"No, you look at him, Dad. He's alive. He's OK. All you got to do is free him."

"He's not OK, Francis. Look how tight the snare is."

He looked down at the rabbit. His father was right, but it was all so unfair, and this unfairness was wrong in a way beyond explanation or understanding. In Francis's oozing tears the rabbit blurred and dissolved into a puddle that wavered and trembled until he could no longer distinguish it from the brown earth. He pushed past his father and started back towards the bridge, stumbling in his haste to escape the weight of a new and unavoidable knowledge that filled the air around him and pressed down on him, smothering him, refusing to let him breathe.

Jackman watched him go. He did not call after him. Eventually, some day, Francis would have no choice but to understand. He turned to the rabbit and knelt beside it. With the edge of his hand he struck its neck and the rabbit shivered and was dead.

Later he would have a talk with the boy. He would explain how obligations chased you down and cornered you, or how you blundered into them and got caught. It was all the same in the end. He would tell him that they were inescapable, no matter how clever or nimble or devious you were, no matter what you planned or hoped for, no matter how fast you ran.

Snares were part of everyone's run, he'd explain. There was no way to escape them without leaving part of yourself behind.

•••

MICHAEL FINN *was born and raised in Grand Falls. He now lives in St. Bernard's-Jacques Fontaine on the Burin Peninsula. He makes the occasional foray into town.*

The Fates

By Adrienne King

Snatched away from a nosy teenage girlfriend, it was spitefully hidden in a cupboard. She sniffed out his Baby Book among his family's photo albums. ("Geez b'y, I only want to see a picture of you in your little footie pajamas.") He had no real interest in the book, neither the content, nor the authors. He was 16 and not concerned with his infant self or his little life before adoption.

But he recognized the book was special and it was his. On his 21st birthday he stumbled upon it and decided to read it. It was his rite of passage into adulthood.

Three authors wrote this book, a biography of his infant life. Three foster mothers each documented his time with them in a journal. The book travelled with him and his clothes and toys to each new home, and finally to his permanent adoptive home. This book was his thread from birth to the beginning of his life with his adopted family. It gave him a history he could share with his own children: "When I was a baby, I crawled everywhere after the dog. One time I almost went out the gate on to Logy Bay Road."

He didn't really remember these foster mothers who eased him into the world. He couldn't remember their lullaby voices, or holding their giant hands with his fingers. But when he read the Greek myth of The Fates, goddess creators of everything, he immediately thought of them. To the Fates, every life is a thread they control. Clotho is the mother and spinner who begins life, Lachesis is the maiden and weaver who develops life, and Atropos is the crone and cutter of the thread who ends life.

His foster mothers were ethereal creatures. He had a vague sense of what they looked like from some blurry photos, but they were more myth than mortal to him. They shaped his infant life, and delivered him to his family, and then returned to their realms.

At 21, he preferred the second author, Lachesis. A scrapbooker, she decorated his milestones with stickers, and pictures, and decorative borders. She cared for him from 10 months old to 15 months. She wrote in glitter pen; curly, girly, smiley letters. Every tooth, every step, every solo sit-up and first bite of carrot were commemorated with fuzzy kittens and heart stickers hugging his photos to the pages. He loved her brash, big affection. She measured love in glitter. It was a slightly crazy section of the journal. It was cuddly chaos and affection overflow. His head was in a similar place and his heart was perpetually on his flashy sleeve. Her voice on the page was sing-songy and cooed, "My little dumplin' sure loves his carrots, oh yes he does. He gobble, gobble, gobbles like a little baby chick." He saw how much love this mother gave him as the little specks reflected light all over his clothes.

Closed with happiness and tucked back into its cupboard, the book waited.

He celebrated his 30th birthday at Blue on Water. He continued his milestone tradition at home later. His belly full of steak and wine, he searched through the last few unpacked boxes for his book. With his book located, and a big glass of chocolate milk poured, he reread it to see which author spoke to him now. It was Atropos, who wrote only the facts. She was his last foster mother, and raised him from 15 months to 20 months. Precise block letters in Bic ballpoint pen documented names, dates and locations.

Photos held themselves on with two-sided tape. Her photos depicted structured activities and were planned, posed shots. No candid, goofy pictures here. She included medical information. "He walks and runs very well, but with a slight bend in his gait. I've had him checked for scoliosis, and he is fine. This may be something to keep an eye on in his teenage years, however." It had a Zen quality to it. He liked how it laid everything bare. At this point in his life, he had no use for emotional sloppiness. He kept everything close to his chest and suffered no sentimentality. This is all I really am, he thought; blood type B, a little myopic, and no known allergies.

Closed crisply, and efficiently placed in its new home on a shelf in the bedroom closet, the book waited.

His 40th was a huge family picnic in Pippy Park. His post-party reading ritual continued. With two small children of his own, he was drawn to the first author, Clotho. Her account was more anecdotal with little daily triumphs. This part of his biography took him from birth to 10 months; around the age of his youngest girl.

This mother wrote in what appeared to be anything that was handy. Some entries were in pen, and some were in marker, and some were the thick lines of a rounded-off crayon. He loved how she described him "reading the paper" with her or that he squealed when she blew on his face. She included photos, but each had a little story instead of dates and places. He could identify the places anyway: Kent's Pond, Bannerman Park. There were all kinds of pictures that showed the soft edges of his life with her. One picture showed her holding him and smiling for the camera while the cat licked his bottle that was sitting on the floor.

The good stuff was the story of each day, like how a dog ran off with his dirty diaper when he was being changed in the park, or how even at seven months, he could pick his favourite book out of a stack. She included things like, "You giggle when you fart and when we laugh at you, you giggle and fart more." Most entries were punctuated with "You are so smart." "You're such a strong boy!" "Everyone loves you!" "I'm so proud to introduce you to everyone!"

This mother had a bit of everyone and some extra stuff thrown in. She was loving and true and a bit out in left field. She spoke to his life right now, and followed him all the way to the present to give him a hug and reassure him he was doing well with his own children.

Closed lovingly and placed on a shelf in the closet of his oldest child, the book waited.

•••

ADRIENNE KING grew up in Corner Brook but spent most of her young adult life in Toronto. She decided to move back during a Christmas night showing of "The Shipping News." She now lives in Portugal Cove-St. Philip's with her husband, Jon, and a host of charming creatures.

The Grocery List

By Melissa Barbeau

The list was stuck to the fridge with one of those stainless steel magnetic canisters. They had ordered them from the Lee Valley catalogue, along with the Citrus Reamer and a set of Lifetime Measuring Cups. They cooked every weekend first when they were married, for friends or just themselves.

The canisters held exotic spices. Cumin, turmeric, saffron. Hungarian paprika. Mace. She was always careful pulling the lids off of them. They were sealed hermetically tight to preserve the freshness of their contents. They resisted being opened and she worried that the two halves would pull apart suddenly, rather than in the controlled way she hoped. They were together so firmly, the two parts of that whole, and she was afraid every time she pulled at it. Every time she tried to put it asunder. Worried that the contents would fly from the container in a dusty cloud around the kitchen, mingling with the dust on the floor so that it was no longer the singular ingredient in a meal that was meant to be lingered over. Calamari risotto blackened with ink. Paella. Curries with crisp samosas and pakoras and naan bread to soak up every drip drop of liquid. Chicken molé, thick with chocolate and chilies. Spices settling like so much fragrant dust amongst the pedestrian dirt that covered the floor. Aromatic as it was swept into the dustpan.

Now the canisters gathered dust. Waiting to be opened like treasure. Gleaming like jewels on the side of the fridge — powdered amber, umber, rust. Gleaming behind the clear acrylic tops while dishes piled up in the sink.

dish detergent

laundry detergent

toilet paper

Now meals were less elaborate. She had nursed the baby for a long time and even though she told herself and her mother and Tim and the pediatrician that "mothers in India ate curries every day!" and "mothers in Mexico ate chilies every day!" and "mothers in Ethiopia ate harissa every day!" the baby was still gassy and fussy and colic and was up all night if she ate spicy food or milk or turnip or chocolate or cabbage or kale or anything leafy and deep, dark, foresty green. And so she weaned herself off anything that upset his belly and he grew big and round and fat, dispelling the notion that breastfed babies were leaner than the ones raised on Carnation milk.

diapers

The disposable diapers fell somewhere between concession and defeat. Idealism meeting the reality of sleep deprivation. She had managed the food a little better. The baby was on solids now, hand-puréed organics.

beets

carrots

parsnips

But by then she was out of the habit of opening the little jars of spices or pounding flat a clove of garlic, and supper was plain rice or a baked potato and a pork chop. And most of the time, by the time she was done boiling and blending locally grown seasonal vegetables into a congealed mush that ended up as much on the floor and in her hair and on the baby's sleeper (staining it beyond saving) as in the baby, all she was interested in was toast.

The colic had been the worst of it, though. It kept her up all night, kept her out of the laundry room, out of the shower. Kept even her most loyal of her friends away most of the time. When they came to visit her and they asked what they could do to help she thrust the red-faced, squalling baby into their arms and went into the other room for a cup of tea.

Tim had started poking down to Christian's for a beer after work and then they were calling up for him for a birthday dinner at the Italian place down the street and there was no way she could go; not with the baby wailing and she wasn't fit anyway, leaking milk through yesterday's pyjamas, stinking of stale sweat. So he went without her and the next thing it was golf and drinks and could you blame him for coming in late smelling of Scotch and collapsing on the couch to sleep it off. Trying not to disturb her in the bed.

She looked at the time. It was getting late not to have heard from him. Nothing on the calendar for tonight; he would have called by now. She tapped the pen on the tabletop. Maybe they could cook a little meal. Nothing elaborate. Now that the baby was on solids he was sleeping most of the night. If she got him down by eight …

She studied the containers clinging forgotten to the side of the fridge. Running through her options.

butter

cod

basmati

A nice white?

Pinot Grigio

She wiped a layer of grime from the lid of the jar she had laid on the table in front of her. How old was this stuff? She eased it open and stuck her nose in the jar.

dill

She looked at the clock and down at herself. Lifted the front of her sweatshirt away from her chest and sniffed. A shower was a necessity.

She'd only have time to pop down to the little grocery store. No time to shop for whatever industrial strength negligee would be necessary to reconstruct her fallen breasts; now that she had stopped nursing they had deflated like two water balloons that had sprung leaks, lost their buoyancy. She was sure she had a matching bra and panties somewhere. She would pull on one of his T-shirts and a pair of his work socks. She ran her hand along her calf.

shaving cream

She was in the bathroom when the phone rang, searching in the cabinet under the sink. Pulling out lotions and potions and body butter and creams with shimmer. She let the machine take the call. The phone was a cordless, who knew where it was. Under the laundry? In between the cushions of the couch? She slid across the cold tiles of the bathroom floor on her hands and knees, poking her head out the door to listen to the message.

Leaned her cheek against the coolness of the doorframe.

Tim's voice resonated through the apartment.

She replaced the jars and potions. Gently closed the louvered doors of the vanity. Padded back to the kitchen table; bare feet sticking to spilled juice. The floor tacky.

The pen hovered above the list. The soft sound of the heel of her hand dragging across the paper as she drew careful lines.

dish detergent

laundry detergent

toilet paper

gripe water

diapers

beets

carrots

parsnips

butter

~~cod~~

~~Basmati~~

~~Pinot Grigio~~

~~dill~~

~~shaving cream~~

macaroni

• • •

MELISSA BARBEAU *is a writer who lives with her husband and four children in foggy Torbay. In her spare time she teaches instrumental music at St. Peter's Junior High in Mount Pearl. She has previously published in Memorial University's literary journal Paragon, online on saltyink.com and this spring won a Newfoundland and Labrador Arts and Letters Award for non-fiction.*

PAM FRAMPTON is associate managing editor and an award-winning columnist with The Telegram. She has a BA (Honours) in English literature from Memorial University of Newfoundland and has worked as a journalist for more than 20 years. Originally from Trinity Bay, she lives in St. John's with her husband, video-journalist Glenn Payette. She is also the editor of volumes I, II, III and IV of *The Cuffer Anthology*.